Letting Paddy Fly

David King

Letting Paddy Fly

Letting Paddy Fly
ISBN 978 1 76041 076 6
Copyright © text David King 2015

First published 2015 by
GINNINDERRA PRESS
PO Box 3461 Port Adelaide 5015
www.ginninderrapress.com.au

Contents

Letting Paddy Fly

She'd sent Paddy a Valentine during the unkind days when he was remote from her, made it herself, pasted hearts and violets on the front, pinked the edges with nail scissors, an act that took her the whole of one wizened Sunday, when even her fire burned cold. She wounded one heart with a silver arrow emblazoned with down she'd extracted from her pillow. Beneath the montage she wrote *Absence makes the fond heart wonder.*

That brought him running to her from whichever sordid labyrinth he'd chosen for his exile. The scuffed mahogany and flaky glass partitions of the office where she spent her weekdays shook as he rushed in like the west wind and grasped her wrists while his eyes transfixed her as if he was Jesus come to answer her prayers.

She told him, 'I'm engaged to be married' and, ignoring the questing eyes and ears of her colleagues, he declared his love for her and begged her to choose him instead.

'Oh, Lizzie,' he said, dolorous now and slowly shaking his head. 'Why didn't you tell me before it got serious?'

'I didn't think you were interested in me,' she said and a small vein in her temple began to throb.

That evening they snatched a half hour in a quiet corner of a local pub before Lizzie caught her bus home.

They were close-tongued until Lizzie said, low-voiced and urgent, 'Do you remember when you kissed me?' She pronounced kissed as if it were the most intimate word in her universe.

Paddy, who had been hunched on his seat, sat upright and gazed at her. Lizzie held her breath but Paddy said nothing until she was forced to breathe again.

'As if I could forget,' he said then and as Lizzie saw an old-remembered light flicker through his eyes she marvelled in the revelation that the kiss possessed him too.

Trysts such as this became her lifeline until warmer months smiled and they could rendezvous in the park, spending Lizzie's lunch breaks lying side by side on sun-kissed grass or holding hands within a bower in the rose garden, giddy from the perfumes of incense and musk as their lips came close, but never touched.

At home each evening in her parents' house, Lizzie listened for the growl of her fiancé's car then watched her mother's fat satisfaction as he crossed their threshold.

'Tim, how lovely to see you.' Always the same tired words, served with an over-staged smile that Lizzie wanted to slap back into her mother's face. Tim was her father's name too but there was no welcome on his homecoming from the city, nothing more than a sigh, of indifference or resentment. Lizzie couldn't decide which was worse.

Tim 'how lovely to see you' would peck her mother's cheeks and take Lizzie to watch him play cricket. When they returned and the house was still, his rubber-sheathed penis would shuffle inside her and fill its little sac, a ritual countenanced by Lizzie since their engagement and which, after the initial thrill from behaving indecently while her mother slept a few yards above, she found lacking in substance.

She became prone to staring at the ceiling during Tim's exertions and wondering if the vague stimulation they provided was worth the indignity of the performance. She began to dwell on the memory of Paddy's Kiss, always capitalised in her mind, elevating it to some ethereal plane far above the reality of mere penetrative sex.

Tim's coital grunts seemed identical to those Lizzie heard him utter as he worked out with weights or pedalled sweaty static miles by exercise bike. The thought crossed her mind that to him her vagina was another facility in his polygym, one that didn't exhaust him too much. Although he remembered to say he loved her, she never felt the truth of the words. He expressed similar sentiments about his BMW and his cricket bat and

Lizzie wondered if she and they occupied the same category in Tim's mind.

With Paddy, she didn't need to wonder. He was hers to bleed raw or cherish, and she was comforted by each nuance of emotion that animated his face as she never quite accepted but never quite rejected him. Lately, although Lizzie had admitted nothing, her waning satisfaction with Tim betrayed itself in other ways and she saw Paddy was becoming ebullient.

One day, Lizzie came to him pouting, her face a cloud of frustration. Mother-in-law presumptive had made complaints, the latest of many, over Lizzie's qualities. 'The old witch called me a besom,' she said, allowing herself an expression of outraged innocence. 'I hate her. She makes me so unhappy.'

'Then for your own sake marry me,' said Paddy.

His will shone out and pierced her, and Lizzie unwrapped a decision she'd reached weeks before.

'I will marry you,' she said then listed her preconditions for this happy event: a house, purchased not rented, detached, furnished to a standard endorsed by the glossier magazines. 'It's no more than Tim would provide.'

Paddy stared at her, deep-eyed, and reminded her that he was poor. 'Love doesn't come ready-packaged,' he said. 'It isn't for sale.'

Lizzie was hollow-mouthed at the reproach and hid her face behind her hands before bringing them down again to squeeze Paddy's. 'Oh, Jesus,' she said. 'What a mercenary cow they've turned me into.'

'Tim, how lovely to see you,' her mother said that evening, then Lizzie told him right there in the hallway that she loved someone else. Tim's mouth opened, closed, wordless for once. He shambled past Lizzie into the sitting room and she heard him uncork her father's malt. She fled upstairs and her mother followed, clumping up the Wilton treads in unlikely haste. Lizzie sat on her bed, pressing a photograph to her chest. It was one of those unsatisfactory shots taken in curtained booths that lurk in the popular chain stores and was of a sun-browned, rather scrawny Paddy, sent to her long ago from Cornwall, where he spent the summer of his first dropout year surfing its treacherous waters.

Her mother wrung her podgy hands and arranged her face to show despair. 'Please tell me it's not him.'

Within no time at all, Lizzie was foundering under sustained broadsides from two mothers, hers distraught at the sufficiency she was discarding, Tim's angry that a wee besom could reject her creation. Tim stood clear of the cannonade but cajoled her with promises.

Paddy, in a straight-faced speech that surprised Lizzie, urged her to disregard everything they said. 'Decisions made under duress aren't decisions at all. Choose your future freely and I'll accept it, whether it includes me or not.'

Feeling browbeaten, even by Paddy, Lizzie was soon unable to decide on anything, freely or otherwise. She fell into fits of weeping then took refuge behind the living room sofa, where she sat rocking and sucking her thumb, defying all attempts to flush her out until her father crawled in on his bony hands and knees and offered her a lollipop. Lizzie stared at him as if he was the crazy one, then laughed as she remembered the last time he had made such an offer. It was one summer when Lizzie was about five or six and Uncle Sam, her mother's over-sweaty brother, was their house guest. When he'd tried to cuddle and kiss her, Lizzie brewed up a tantrum and locked herself in the cupboard under the stairs. Her father had coaxed her out with a strawberry lollipop.

'Strawberry, please,' Lizzie said now, standing up and allowing herself to be hugged.

She also allowed herself to be sent to Plas Mawr, a health farm in North Wales, on no stronger recommendation than it was the boyhood home of her father's father. 'A private house then, of course,' her father said, resurrecting Welsh cadences he had long buried.

There, Lizzie stared from a high window for hour upon hour at the high moor that now stretched to the limits of her vision. It was a grey world she saw, tinged with the slate never far beneath its surface and the building that incarcerated her was greyest of all, hewn from its landscape, its birthplace now a water-filled depression thirty yards away. Lizzie wondered how many of her ancestors had drowned themselves there.

As if the moor had power to lull her mind, such melancholy thoughts came less and less to Lizzie and, taking tentative walks, she discovered beauty in her surroundings, like the blithely nodding white fluffs of cotton grass she found amongst pools of blanket bog.

One week in July, she was spellbound as the drab moorland brightened into a sea of purple-pink waves that shimmered in the sun as the wind bent the renascent heather. She thrilled to the joyous summer serenade of skylarks and worried at the ki-ki-ki of a small falcon she watched chasing them through the air, twisting and turning while Lizzie prayed for their safety.

She pretended Plas Mawr was still her grandfather's house and she was visiting him for the summer, with his permission to go where and do as she pleased. He'd died before she was born and Lizzie had never seen his photograph but she pictured him as somewhat like her father, yet happier and perhaps rotund.

Waiting for her indoors were over-long daily sessions with an unsmiling man in a brown suit. Lizzie found them debilitating compared with exploring the moor but consoled herself with the thought that he was at least someone to talk to, for her fellow inmates only exhibited vacuous smiles, the nurses were taciturn, and the domestics always switched from English to Welsh whenever she came close.

On Sundays, though, there was too much talk. Lizzie's parents visited then and her mother impressed on her what a silly girl she was and how she mustn't waste her future on someone who didn't have two halfpennies to rub together and would more than likely end up in prison, or worse if they still hanged people.

In sentences punctuated only by eloquent sighs from Lizzie's father, she peppered Lizzie with the virtues of an income that would release her from semi-detacheds and wet fortnights in Yarmouth and washing the Rover each Sunday. Tim was a honeymoon in Mauritius and houses with grounds and yachts in the Med and running the Merc through the car wash. That waste-of-space on the other hand was a basement flat with cockroaches or a council house if she was lucky, and waiting for the bus and queuing for the dole and fish and chips on a Friday.

A rational Lizzie could withstand these verbal marathons but during the sixth visitation, her brain began to sizzle and she knew it would burst if she heard one further manic word. She shrieked at her mother, 'All right, all right, I'll marry Tim if that will only shut you up.'

When she and Tim were reunited, he smiled as if he'd expected her capitulation all along and she redeemed a morsel of lost dignity by slapping his face. He laughed it off but she saw a sliver of uncertainty wedge into his self-confidence.

She had no defences, however, against Paddy's damp-eyed reaction to her defection and she snapped at him, 'Pull yourself together.'

His cheeks blazed as if she had slapped them too.

She phoned him next day and said she was sorry and he seemed to accept the way things were. On her final day at work, they drank Asti spumante together and Paddy serenaded her with 'Halfway to Paradise'. Lizzie felt a perversely comforting ache beneath her ribs as she heard Paddy wail that he wanted to be her lover, but her friend was all he stayed. She ordered repeat performances until someone said, 'For Christ's sake let him die in peace.'

Unwilling in the end to let him go, she cushioned Paddy against her breast while Tim loitered, head turned away, on the opposite side of the street. 'Promise me, Paddy,' she said, 'that you won't turn up at the wedding.'

Paddy's eyes narrowed. 'To speak out or for ever hold my peace?'

Lizzie watched his mouth tighten and wished she had chosen different words.

Paddy gazed at the sky and his lips moved silently as if in secret prayer. When he turned back to her, his eyes had their old sparkle and he smiled in such a beatific way that she felt she'd been granted absolution. 'Don't fret, Lizzie,' he said. 'I won't turn up at the wedding.'

But he did turn up at her gate as she stepped out in white silk and lace, arm in arm with her top-hatted and morning-suited father. Lizzie pressed a hand to her mouth as she saw him swaying amongst a cohort of oohing and aahing neighbours.

'Doesn't he understand,' she asked her father when they were safely in the bridal car, 'that he mustn't see the bride before the wedding?'

'But you're marrying Tim, not him,' said her father.

Lizzie said nothing.

They didn't honeymoon in Mauritius but the Bahamas were nearly as good, said Tim. He took his golf clubs along and spent much of his time hitting balls in company with business clients while Lizzie waited at the nineteenth hole and sipped turbid drinks from frosted glass.

Her new home was a box of startling red bricks, four en suites and a three-car garage. Lizzie supposed the bricks would mellow in time. Within insulated walls, she dusted and vacuumed then prepared Tim's dinner for six o'clock. Dizzied by gastronomic directions, she'd fret over synchronising each ingredient but Tim never commented on her results, only prattled away about bottom lines and such, things he'd never mentioned before their marriage. Lizzie smiled and nodded and said things like 'Oh, really?' when Tim paused for her reaction, but she didn't understand a word he said.

She learned from her mother that Paddy had got into trouble on the evening of her wedding day. It seemed that someone said the wrong words and Paddy went for him with the pig stabber end of a jackknife. Palpably drunk in the morning, he must have been paralytic by then, thought Lizzie. Anyway he'd missed, thank God, and only impaled a fencepost. Fists, though, carried the argument further and Paddy's earned him three months for assault. 'There,' said Lizzie's mother, wagging a freshly glossed finger at her. 'I told you he'd end up in jail.'

Lizzie wept on Paddy's behalf but also tingled within at the concept that, even if not in shining armour, he'd acted like a champion of old defending her, his lady. She imagined him carrying her favour secreted close to his heart, a fragment of intimate lace perhaps. She decided to enquire about visiting hours.

Paddy's welfare, however, was soon suspended in favour of her own.

That evening, Tim carried a furtive look about him, like a boy caught reading dirty magazines. Over dinner, which for the first time she had forgotten to cook and so was the result of a hurried visit to a takeaway, he suddenly said, 'It would be rather nice if you were pregnant.'

Lizzie liked her current figure and thought her womb was best left untested. She snapped at Tim, saying 'rather nice' wasn't her view actually. She suspected his agenda was downloaded from his mother, who'd taken to landing on her by taxi on afternoons when she wasn't playing bridge. She'd peer beneath furniture and tut about 'empty bedrooms' with a vulture's glint that Lizzie knew meant business.

When even her own mother began gushing about babies, Lizzie screamed, 'Christ, I wish I was locked up like Paddy.' To Paddy's photograph, which she kept as a bookmark inside her bedtime reading, she said, 'I'm sorry I haven't visited but you're better off without me.'

After putting herself on the pill, she allowed Tim to dispense with his nightly condom. She maintained her deception for months but one morning he waved the incriminating package at her. 'Ma was looking for something to ease her headache.' Lizzie had kept them in her knickers drawer beneath pristine white layers.

Lizzie carried for three months then lost the baby. As her grief spilt and spread inside her, Tim breezed into the private room he and Ma had insisted on and said, 'Don't worry, darling, we can try for another soon.'

She wanted to yell at him, 'It's my dead baby, not a broken BMbloodyW' but she adopted a wan smile instead. Until he went away.

Tim tried for another with a determination that left Lizzie reeling. Each evening, as the clock ticked towards bedtime, she found herself inventing elaborate reasons for incapacity, which Tim circumvented by ignoring them.

After her fourth miscarriage in fifteen months and mounds of dried tears, Lizzie finally said, 'No more.'

She expected bluff and bluster but Tim, peering into her face more closely than she could recall him doing before, said 'Okay', so softly she could scarcely hear him.

When he had gone, she looked at her reflection in the mirror of her compact. A wraithlike creature stared back at her through dark-rimmed eyes, and for a moment she wondered who it was.

After a few weeks superficial fussing over her, Tim began to work late, sometimes arriving home accompanied by a guilty smile. After smarting over the first few occurrences, Lizzie felt an increasing indifference at the prospect of his infidelity.

Soon, his mother claimed to have suffered a stroke.

'Ma's vulnerable alone,' Tim said, 'and we have empty rooms.' He drummed his fingers as he spoke and Lizzie winced at the stress he laid on empty.

Ma moved in and Lizzie diluted the new presence with gin and Mahler. One morning, when the CD player refused to work, she switched the television on instead, strayed from a chat show into BBC2 and discovered an Open University broadcast about the changing role of women.

'It's a lot of money,' she said but Tim seemed to want to indulge her.

He threw his arms extravagantly aside. 'It'll keep you out of mischief,' he said.

Lizzie wondered what mischief he'd been into.

Ma muttered about education and cranky besoms being incompatible but, for once, Tim predominated and Lizzie began an arts course.

'I must get my TMA to my tutor by the end of the week,' she said whenever Tim complained about microwaved convenience food and his lack of manicured shirts. His rebukes were too bland and Lizzie waited for a major eruption.

To her surprise, Ma provided an escape route by adopting an indulgent smile and saying, 'It's just as well someone has a pair of hands.'

At the university summer school, Lizzie allowed herself to be seduced by her philosophy tutor, whose lank dark hair and mysterious eyes reminded her too much of Paddy. As part of her course, she'd been studying ancient Celtic society and was fascinated by the right of 'thigh-freedom' whereby, without stigma, iconic women like Isolde, Guinevere and Boudicca could open their legs to males of their choice. In the high that the week's concentrated brainstorms, bacchanals and beautiful people had brought on in her, she decided that, as she was half-Celtic, such thigh-friendships applied to her too.

When he'd returned to her, after the Valentine, Paddy had said he'd always loved her. 'Yet you did nothing about it,' she'd said. Well, Paddy, she thought, her eyes screwed tight as she imagined it was him inside her, you're doing something now. And as the philosopher quivered and ejaculated, Lizzie cried, 'Fuck me, Paddy, fuck me!' and blushed mentally as deed and words rammed the pinch-point of her conscience.

'By the bye,' the philosopher said as Lizzie zipped up her jeans, 'My name isn't Paddy.'

'I was sublimating,' said Lizzie and the philosopher's grin dissolved.

After summer school she switched from arts to psychology academically and at home, then renewed Tim's access to her body. He grinned as if he was opening bat at Lords and Lizzie's baby girl, golden-haired like her, was born the following April, prematurely as far as Tim was concerned. Lizzie named her Patricia and hoped he wouldn't follow connections.

Although, to Tim's regularly expressed dismay, there were no more babies, with Ma safely fettered as self-appointed nanny, Lizzie gained her further credits with distinction and was awarded a first-class degree. In view of the unplanned results of summer school, she was always careful to select courses that didn't involve one. She didn't mention this to Tim, however, so for a week or so each June she was free to remove herself from garish suburban bricks to marvel at magical, yet undemanding things such as white crests on restless seas or multifaceted panoramas viewed from high hills.

She'd taken to hiding her contraceptives with her dirty knickers, knowing Ma was squeamish about such things. Patricia, though, had no such inhibitions and one day Tim found her trying to post the pills into the unyielding mouth of a Barbie doll.

Lizzie's mother clucked and fussed like a tetchy chicken. 'Bruises are part of marriage, dear. Get used to them.'

Lizzie was open-mouthed at the prospect of her weedy father attempting fisticuffs against such solid opposition. But it was he, an unlikely Sir Lancelot, who stood as Lizzie's new champion. He brushed his moustache and arranged his hair to cover some scalp then galloped off in the Rover with her.

'How dare you assault my daughter,' he raged at Tim, gesticulating at the darkening contusions on Lizzie's face. Stretching higher than she thought possible, he placed a careful uppercut under his son-in-law's chin then, clutching Lizzie's hand, marched with almost military élan back to his car.

Lizzie was reminded then of the medals, one a cross with a white and purple ribbon that, during the summer when she'd hidden under the stairs, she'd found in an old shoebox there.

The Rover's departure was more sedate than its arrival, and Lizzie watched Tim, up to then expressionless, twist his features into a fury and bang his forehead against a door jamb. She caught a momentary glimpse of Ma hovering behind him in the shadows but of Patricia there was no sign.

Tim flurried Lizzie with flowers, entreaties to come home. He couldn't stand much more of Ma, and Patricia was siding with her and, well, he just couldn't cope. He said nothing about loving Lizzie, of missing her. Even so, she became exasperated with her own mother's fluttering and endless rash generalisations, and might well have given in if Paddy hadn't joined the conversation one evening.

Her father was treating himself to a pipe before doing the washing up. 'Here, isn't this that chap you used to hang around with?' he said, waving the evening paper in the air. 'The one that was mooching outside on your wedding day?'

There was a quarter-page photograph of Paddy wearing a suit and looking as if he'd scooped the prizes at speech day. As he had in a way, winning the local university's award for a doctoral thesis in philosophy. She knew he'd studied international politics before he first dropped out but Paddy a philosopher! Who would believe it? Was his metamorphosis,

Lizzie wondered, because, in losing me, he discovered himself? He was described as the most exciting prospect the department had discovered in years.

She felt a rush of affection for him combined with a heady sense of pride. Recalling her daughter's conception, she had a wild fancy that Patricia really was Paddy's, inseminated by transubstantiation via one philosopher to another. 'Our baby, Paddy,' she cried. 'I must get our baby back.'

Her father knocked his pipe out in the hearth, and cradled her in his arms until she stopped palpitating and became a child again, cocooned once more in a comforting aroma of Edgeworth tobacco.

He suggested she try Plas Mawr again and Lizzie smiled, remembering purple heather and the merlin chasing the skylarks. A lifetime ago.

'Just rest and recuperation this time, no shrinks,' her father said. 'Heaven knows, you've read all the books.' He winked at her. 'Oh, and no visits from your mother.' His eyes were blue steel as he directed them at his wife, who lowered hers in unaccustomed acquiescence.

Lizzie met Paddy, almost bumped into him, two days before leaving for North Wales. She'd braved a trip to town to supplement the clothes she was wearing. Her father offered to accompany her but knowing he felt nervous in lingerie departments she said, 'No, I'll be all right. Really.'

She was in the queue for the till in Marks and Spencer when she saw Paddy approaching. Her heart leaped in telltale spasms as she prepared to dump her selections and dash for the escalator. Then she noticed Paddy's armful of gaudy ties, silk she thought, and the contrast with his washed out T-shirt and knee-holed Levis made her stop and shake her head instead.

Paddy looked rueful but his eyes were twinkling. 'They're for a new job,' he said. 'Not really me, are they?'

He seemed taller somehow, although Lizzie knew that was impossible. 'I've left Tim,' she said. 'I'm going away for a while.'

Paddy nodded, his face instantly serious. 'I'm sorry,' he said. 'Truly.'

Lizzie had reached the head of the queue by then and, as she handed over her purchases, Paddy said, 'I still remember it.'

The cashier said, 'Fifty-three ninety-five.'

Lizzie was studying Paddy's face. 'Me too,' she said, as the cashier coughed and said, 'Would you sign this, please?'

As Lizzie took the voucher from the cashier, Paddy dipped a hand in a back pocket of his jeans and came up with a crumpled business card. He took the pen that the cashier was now offering Lizzie and scribbled on the card. 'Call me,' he said, handing Lizzie the card and pen. 'When you're able to. No strings.'

The winds gusting around Plas Mawr carried more than a breath of winter but Lizzie rarely stayed indoors, preferring to make solitary excursions along the network of footpaths around what she now thought of simply as her grandfather's house.

In this way, she discovered an inn that stood like a sentinel at the highest point of the road crossing the moor. She was surprised to find it bubbling with conversations of van and lorry drivers: Welsh, Scots, Geordie, Brum, Scouse, Cockney and the estuary-speak of younger men, curiously homogeneous whatever their geographical origins. The discordant mix suited her and she found she could enjoy the yearning looks, ignore the lascivious offers.

She sat in a corner with a notebook and pen and wrote down whatever filtered through her head. Most days, little of consequence was noted, some days nothing at all. But on her sixth visit, Lizzie wrote down, *Some moments, some meetings are so intense. They may appear to be a simple conversation, a transient exchange, but beneath such wrappings is an event that consummates each soul. In circumstances such as these, a kiss can be more penetrating than the wildest sex. It was like that with the man I didn't marry.*

She sat gazing at her words for a full hour, her body taut, her breathing barely perceptible, until a worried-looking barman asked her if she was all right.

'Yes, I believe I am now, thank you,' she said, then rose and left the inn for the last time.

Back in her room at Plas Mawr, she chose a ladder-backed chair rather than the chesterfields gracing each side of the fireplace. Unravelling experiences that really mattered required alertness, not comfort. She opened her notebook and mused over the words she had written in the inn.

On their first date, she and Paddy hadn't even kissed. Close enough together in the back row but with Paddy ramrod-backed until she'd grabbed his right arm and pulled it around her shoulders. Their friendship flourished from then on but Paddy's romantic demonstrations were still best described as lukewarm.

Why? She'd known what he did with his other girlfriends, so why not her? It wasn't as if she wasn't desirable. Back then. She'd had a good figure, voluptuous some said, and Paddy couldn't have missed it in the fitted dresses she liked to wear.

But their last date: that was perfect from the start. It followed a short period of estrangement when she and he looked elsewhere. Both straight from work (he'd had a job then) and onto the bus, he'd been in a wonderful humour, full of vitality and she was glowing, expectant of good things happening, as if she'd been granted the keys to Eden. The conductor seemed to pick up their mood and served jests all the way to their stop but Paddy's returns were devastating and Lizzie bubbled with unquenchable glee. In the cinema, Paddy bought chocolates but they didn't open them. Never saw the film either. For its entire three-hour run, they were locked in one marvellous embrace. Paddy started it, kneading his lips against hers, savouring, exploring, urgent, and she had reciprocated with equal enthusiasm. They never became sore or dry and Lizzie couldn't imagine how they managed to breathe. She didn't remember tongues.

She could smell their clean sweat and feel the heat of their bodies now, as real as if they were physically together in this room. Half-closing her eyes to visualise their actions in soft focus, she saw their hands trace their way through each other's hair and about their upper bodies and yes, his did find her breasts, she hadn't been sure before. And again she experienced the exquisite, numinous feeling that had pulsated through her then, and knew that it was happening to him at that exact moment, wherever he might be. She even had a name for it: orgasm by psychokinesis.

They'd been last to leave the cinema and they staggered along its aisles like drunks. They ate the chocolates when they got outside and that rush of sugar gave them enough energy to reach the bus station. Paddy had wanted to take her home. She said, 'There's no point, Paddy,' and saw something die in his eyes. She knew she should have said 'Yes' even if it meant smuggling him into the house and doing it on the carpet where, years later, Tim exercised his pleasure. She knew that now.

Paddy never gave another sign that he wanted more than friendship. Sometimes she'd glimpse hidden meanings behind his layers of banter and wish she could bulldoze through the veneer. She persevered for three years then he backed off entirely. Apart from third-hand tales of drinking and rutting, she heard no more of him or from him until, on God knows what whim, she sent the Valentine.

She'd brought Paddy's photograph to Plas Mawr and she picked it up as she rose from her chair and crossed to the window. She unlocked the catch and lowered the upper sash. A fair breeze was blowing and she watched it shiver over the funereal water in the old quarry. She would count to ten then let the wind carry Paddy's photograph where it would.

If it chose the lake, then she was all done with him, but if it landed on the ground, then she wasn't. She realised that life decisions required more input than this but was wary of initiating the logical moves. No, more than that – she was terrified. And knowing that, at last she understood Paddy's own reticence. Well, she thought, between them a doctor of philosophy and a psychology major ought to be capable of resurrecting what should never have been lost.

She knew that the odds were in favour of him missing the water.

But she let Paddy fly just the same.

I Saw You Dance at Radio City

In a small town at the back end of Alabama, Connie sits at a bar beside a half-empty glass of Chardonnay.

On the dance floor, couples slide and sway to a country waltz oozing from a silver Wurlitzer. Between them and Connie, people sit at round tables: talking, laughing, sometimes crying. Smoke drifts from cigarettes and cheroots, floats over everyone in somnolent clouds.

Connie, mouth half-open, watches the dancing. Each time the music stops, she tells a story, fluttering her eyelids as she speaks. Nobody's in range except the good ole boys drinking beer at the end of the bar, rubbing their fat asses against its mahogany. They crack jokes about Connie that start off whispered but gain volume with each round.

She closes her ears, clings to her stories until the music begins again.

Connie lives downtown in a three-room walk-up flat. At six o'clock every evening, her routine is to go to her old Victor stereo, remove the Sinatra album she's been playing on and off all day, and replace it with *West Side Story*, the Hollywood version. She listens to it for half an hour then prepares her bath.

On her bathroom wall is a faded card that says 'Cleanliness is next to Godliness'. She's had that a long time, remembers the Little Sisters of St Therese presenting it to her but not the where or the why.

Connie mouths the card's aphorism then fills her bath with nine inches of tepid water, checks the depth with a boxwood rule. By now the first side of *West Side Story* has finished, so Connie returns to the stereo, flips the album over.

She spends just four minutes bathing then transfers to her bedroom, sits in an old Lloyd Loom chair to apply her make-up. The silvering on her dressing table mirror has frittered edges, making Connie's pale, freckled face appear in the glass like a vignette.

Marni Nixon's voice filters through with 'I Feel Pretty'. Connie sings along with it, paints her lipstick on, dreamy-eyed, relaxed about where it starts or stops, and when she switches to her hair, doesn't notice the split ends.

On Connie's dressing table are a silver candlestick and a silver jewellery box. One day each year, although she can't explain why, even less say what date, Connie feels moved to take a candle from the jewellery box, place it in the candlestick. It stays, unlit, for twenty-four hours, then Connie returns it to the box. The candle is white, scented with something faintly ecclesiastical. Connie thinks the Little Sisters of St Therese might have given that to her too.

Grooming completed, Connie puts on the red strappy dress she wears whether it is summer or winter. Meanwhile, *West Side Story* plays on and as the last notes of 'Somewhere' fade, Connie sighs, turns the stereo off, slips her feet into her only pair of evening shoes. Both the dress and shoes bear Milanese labels.

At eight p.m., Connie leaves her flat, clutching an embroidered silk evening bag. She takes a cab to the bar, doesn't tip the driver.

That is her routine, and tonight was no exception.

A stranger appears beside Connie. He's around twenty-five, with a dark forest of hair combed back in waves. He has an Italian look, aquiline, a hint of stubble.

He asks Connie to dance. He has an East Coast accent.

Connie ignores him. Like the good ole boys' jokes, she's used to this approach too, to the hooting laughter as she is abandoned in the middle of the floor.

But this young man seems to be alone. He repeats his invitation until Connie finally accepts.

They take the floor to yet another waltz. Connie's first steps are uncertain but her partner leads well, and from somewhere she finds a fluidity of movement she feels she must have lost a long, long time ago in a place far removed from this.

She closes her eyes. Suddenly – it comes like a thunderbolt - she recalls being nineteen. It was her first ball and, yes, she was dancing with a young man much like this one. And the music, oh the music – that was nothing like this – almost glided her around the floor without her even trying. That was how it all started…

Connie's memory gets hazy and she doesn't know what it was that started. She has vague impressions of a wedding that may not have been hers, for she doesn't remember love. What she does recall are tears, a railroad train, a thousand miles of track.

Connie imagines she is floating. The other dancers have stopped. She glimpses them, standing at the sides of the floor, mouths hanging. Even the good ole boys have moved away from the bar. Nobody is laughing at her now.

The music ends and someone starts to clap. Soon every pair of hands in the room is joining in.

'I saw you dance at Radio City.'

Connie shivers; she stares at the young man for a full minute. There can't possibly have been a child. Surely she could never forget something like that.

'You're confusing me with someone else,' she says at last. 'I've never been to New York. Never been a dancer.'

The young man frowns. Connie sees something flicker across his eyes.

'You do know who I am?' He's gripping her hands.

Connie's eyes glaze over. 'Yes,' she says. 'You're someone who came in here by mistake.'

The young man steps back. His mouth clenches. Connie sees his brow straining, senses a struggle inside his head.

He starts to say something then stops, begins again, 'Is that really all you have to say?'

'No, of course not.' Connie smiles, stretches up to peck his cheek. 'Thank you very much for the dance. I've had a lovely evening.'

She reclaims her seat at the bar, picks up her glass, starts to hum a lullaby. She thinks it might be candle-day tomorrow.

Who will look after the roses?

Karolyi suspects it isn't the most sensible thing to do, give a recital in the middle of the city's main street, even when the traffic has died.

He lifts his cello from its battered brown case and sits, legs apart, on his fold-out patio chair. The cello fills the void between his thighs.

Others will paint the pictures, write the words, but Karolyi knows he must look after the music. He wonders who will look after the roses.

Roses worry him. Once they were things to enjoy: weaving sensuous spells through lush gardens, raising delicate petals to greet the sun.

Karolyi recalls summer afternoons: Dvořák's Cello Concerto played al fresco in city parks, supported by a symphony of perfumes from albas, gallicas, damasks, musks and, his favourite of all, Rosa primula, the incense rose. These are things he is sure of.

Then (he can't say why it happened) roses stopped reaching for the sun and began to form their petals in cold concrete. And their thorns tore heads and limbs away from bodies that needed them.

He first witnessed this on the day he missed his last tram. Karolyi could see people waiting to board but running with his cello wasn't easy and he decided to let the tram go. As he relaxed, something fell from the sky and blew the queue he should have been part of into the summer air. Karolyi was still more than a hundred metres away and, as slivers of God knows what hit his cello case, caught in his hair and coloured his clothes, he crumpled to his knees and vomited into the gutter.

He forgot about going home, lived where he worked, at the philharmonic hall. When that became rubble, he and some colleagues gave concerts in ruined houses, anywhere people dared to gather, but never in the open air. Karolyi slept in cellars and doorways, always with his cello wedged safely behind him.

Weeks passed before he felt able to revisit the tram stop and when he did, he saw roses etched into the pavement where the passengers had stood. He understood the implication immediately. In future, he must play his music among these flowers of the streets, because those of concerts in civic parks were finished.

The first time he unfolded his chair, someone said, 'You crazy fool, sitting there in the street. Don't you understand? There's a war going on.'

Karolyi looked up, saw a thin man gesticulating, and began to play Brahms. He fancied he could smell incense burning.

Karolyi dreams that one day someone will paint rose colours into these concrete petals. Blush pink and primrose yellow to ivory white, all the subtle shades between?

No. Red, he thinks. They will be blood red. He doesn't understand why that conclusion saddens him.

In the city around him, eye-searing flashes precede stentorian thunderclaps and buildings collapse like the playing-card houses he might have built as a child. These new fireworks are a thousand times brighter and noisier than those he thinks he remembers from New Year's Eve.

'Sniper!' someone shouts and people scatter as swarms of great bees buzz along the street and ricochet from buildings.

Karolyi stays where he is. He doesn't mind bees; they fertilise the roses.

Now and then he hears what might be screams. He chooses the adagio from Beethoven's Cello Sonata No. 5. Sometimes he forgets its name, but he never forgets the music. It was what he always played at the close of a concert and it drowns out every other sound and thought from his head.

Someone applauds from a deep doorway. Karolyi bows briefly before placing his cello back in the brown case. He folds his chair and, chin high, marches across the street to a military tune that haunts his mind.

He walks down steps to a small café. Its windows are at street level. Inside, there is no electric light, only candles. 'Table for one,' he says to a waitress who sits on a tall stool.

She shrugs and waves her arms at the empty room. Karolyi looks around. Each table wears a chequered cloth. Blue and white. Karolyi thinks blue is his favourite colour. He sits with his back to a wall, facing the door.

The waitress comes to take his order. She is black-haired, tiny, with big dark eyes that Karolyi imagines he has seen somewhere else.

'We have burgers,' she says.

Karolyi nods. 'Mutton?' he says.

'You don't want to know,' the waitress says.

The burger comes with French fries and a bottle of beer. Karolyi can hear noises somewhere. The waitress shuts the windows and draws the curtains. She shivers, folds her arms, pulls them tightly against her sparrow chest.

As Karolyi eats and drinks, the noises become louder and he hears them walk up the street. The café windows shake and he knows there will be roses outside. He looks for the waitress and sees her crouching beneath a table in a corner, as far away from the windows as it is possible to be. An older woman has joined her; she wears a grubby apron and Karolyi assumes she is the cook. Both women are trembling.

Karolyi lifts his cello from its case. He plays his Beethoven adagio.

At last it is quiet, inside and outside.

The waitress smiles as she collects Karolyi's empty plate. 'They've given up early tonight,' she says. 'Your music was beautiful. I think it's charmed them away.'

Karolyi pays his bill. The waitress's dark eyes look hungry as she sees the money in his wallet: deutschmarks, not worthless local paper, a legacy from his last tour. She looks directly into Karolyi's eyes, asks unsaid questions. He nods, and when the café closes, they leave together.

Her name is Dina and she lives in a shell-shocked village that once housed Olympians. Inside her apartment, each window hole is covered in polythene. Karolyi props his cello and chair against an inside wall.

'I won't be long,' Dina says.

Karolyi removes his scuffed shoes, shabby suit, black bow tie, and frilled shirt and hangs them carefully over rusting bed rails. He hears water somewhere and presently Dina rejoins him. She carries her clothes, folded into a neat pile, places them on the only chair. Her eyes seem larger and darker than before; Karolyi cannot tell whether she is excited or frightened.

'Love me,' she says.

They lie on the cold white linen of her bed and as they press themselves into each other, both begin to cry.

Karolyi's home is somewhere he cannot reach any more. There's probably someone he misses, who may miss him in return, but he can't be certain. Sometimes he's not even sure his name is Karolyi, only that people said it was.

Each day, he works the streets. His deutschmarks are gone but he will accept no money for his music. 'Music must be free,' he says but in the evening he sits in the café, eats burgers Dina pays for, then allows himself to play for his supper. And each night he cries when Dina holds him. She doesn't cry any more.

Karolyi sees something new glimmer in Dina's eyes. She hums a gentle tune he doesn't know, seems to expect more from him, but what it might be she does not say. He cannot explain the reason for this change in her; the fireworks carry on as usual and roses still stalk the streets.

Foreigners fly in from somewhere safe. They want Karolyi to form a string quartet with three of his former colleagues. They will fly them out of the city to perform in foreign cathedrals, but then they must return. A deal has been worked out with those who control such things.

Dina frowns when Karolyi explains. 'But you will come back?' she says. She holds a linen dishcloth in her hands, twists it around and around.

'Of course I'll come back,' Karolyi says. 'What would I do without you?'

Dina stands on the perimeter of the pockmarked airport. Karolyi sees her wipe her eyes then wave a slow goodbye as the small aircraft taxis along the only serviceable runway.

They don't have far to fly, a few hundred kilometres to a city once in

Karolyi's own country. Here the roses still grow in gardens. Here they have people to look after them. Karolyi walks with his cello along the streets. They are alive with traffic and Karolyi knows it would truly be madness to play Beethoven in the midst of all this rush.

He drinks coffee until it is time to return to the airport. The café has blue and white checks on the tablecloths and he likes the way the dark-haired waitress smiles. He thinks of his café, of Dina. Why, with a bit of imagination, this could be the same place, the same girl. He dips a hand in his pocket, wraps fingers around money Dina gave him, asks this smiling girl to count it for him.

'Can you play that?' she says, nodding at his case.

'A little,' he says.

He leaves the girl a tip.

In the departure hall, Karolyi's fellow musicians stare at nothing while the foreigners search faces, tap their feet, compare their watches with the big clock on the wall. It suddenly occurs to Karolyi that if this trip could make any difference at all, it would never have been allowed to happen. He steps behind a pillar and keeps it between him and the others as he retreats towards an exit.

He watches the big airplane lift off, carrying three-quarters of the string quartet to a temporary freedom.

He walks back to the café. The waitress's smile is wider than before. This time she comes out from behind her counter and he sees she is plumper, more comfortable than Dina. She brings him coffee and he gives her more of Dina's money.

Karolyi opens his case and takes out his cello. He thinks he might stay here.

Stratherran no more...

Today they are burning our homes. The hollow ring of laughter mocks the braesides as the laird's men pull at thatch and push at turf until, long before noon, only my father's granite walls remain. As they set the torch to our roofs and few sticks of furniture, the men's exuberance mingles with the smoke of our dispossession and both curl upwards to taint the heather where I lie, high on the slopes of Carn Mor.

My parents are gone across the ocean but I shall not follow. When I am stronger, I shall travel south to my mother's people. There men might look at me with more than lust in their eyes and I shall smile at them for the sake of my children that must be born.

Sheep were the cause of our sorrows. I saw my first eleven years ago, on the day I set out for Inverness. The evening before, as we feasted on a fine fish, my father stretched his arms as wide as they would go and proclaimed, 'Our salmon are famous as far as Inverness.' He was proud that we ate the food of kings, though I suppose we were little better off than our neighbours.

I was seven years old and had never considered a world outside Stratherran. I looked up and said, 'How far is Inverness?'

Father tickled me under the chin. 'Oh, the far side of Carn Mor, Maggie.'

I couldn't sleep for thinking about Inverness and next morning sneaked away while Mother and Marie were busy in the kitchen and Father was out on men's business. I had to pause for breath more often than not as I weaved through the rich heather that cloaked the mountain but at last was looking into the glen beyond Carn Mor. But instead of the people and houses I expected, all I saw was a mass of grubby-white creatures blanketing everything but a few patches of green. Was this all there was to Inverness? How could our salmon be famous here?

I half-walked, half-slid into the glen. All around me milled these great fluffy beasts but what struck me most was their smell. Unlike the sweet scents of cows, it stung my nostrils and made my eyes stream. One beast, curly-horned and larger than the rest, glared with red-veined eyes, made a loud quavering noise and stamped a foot at me. I ran for the braeside and home.

'Wherever have you been, Maggie?' Mother sounded cross but I could see the relief in her eyes.

I explained about Inverness.

She hugged me then lifted me up on her lap. 'You're a wee besom, Maggie. So you've had your first acquaintance with sheep?'

I screwed up my nostrils. 'But where were the people, Mammy?'

'Gone,' she said. 'To make room for the sheep.'

'But why did they not send the sheep away?'

Mother frowned and I thought how old she looked. 'When your father's father was young, Maggie, the great sheep were brought up from Argyll. The men marched to drive them back south but their chiefs turned them homeward again.'

'Did they not try again, Mammy?'

'No, Maggie.' Mother's voice became bitter. 'The men could not bear to be disloyal so they left their homes and sailed off obediently to America. Now Stratherran is the only glen free from the sheep.'

'While I am alive,' I said, puffing my chest out, forgetting my flight of that morning, 'the great sheep will never trample Stratherran.'

Mother laughed, and her voice lightened. 'That's my girl, Maggie. Who needs sons with a daughter like you?'

Eight years later, Stratherran was still sheep-free but on the eve of my fifteenth birthday Father came in, grey as the gathering mist outside. He had a paper in his hand and slumped into his chair, called for whisky. 'Sit down, Beth,' he said to Mother. He drank his glass in one swallow, filled it again. 'Five hundred years we have lived in this strath,' he fumed, turning the colour of mulberry. He flung the paper down.

Mother picked it up. 'Forbidden from taking the salmon, the deer, the blackcock and grouse?' As she read, her expression changed from confusion to panic. 'Our bairns need more than tatties and poor greens. The laird will stop us from drinking the water next, or breathing God's fresh air.' She clutched Father's arm. 'John, you must put a stop to this.'

Father shook her away, glared at her. When he spoke, his voice was colder than winter rain. 'He's my chieftain, Beth. What would you have me do? Cut his throat like one of your MacGregors?'

Mother's face became granite but I could feel the hurt in her voice. 'There was never cause to insult my family, John.'

Father sniffed. 'Then why ask when you know I am powerless? At least,' he said, after comforting himself with more whisky, 'the laird's income from our rents and his new sporting customers will keep the sheep away.'

My mother snorted. 'I'm thinking there are plenty of two-legged sheep in the strath already.'

Cattle prices were good that year and on the day our beasts went to market we were expecting Father to return merry with the whisky. But as he walked through our door, his face was ashen.

'It's come at last,' he said. There was no emotion in his voice, no display of fury. He refused dinner, drank deep of the bottle.

Mother shushed Marie and me away to bed early, leaving Father half-senseless stretched across our table. We were afraid to leave our room next morning but Father had already left with the other tacksmen (and what my mother described as 'a very sorry head') to see the laird's factor.

Each half-hour, Mother would have us check the chickens. Meanwhile, she fussed about endlessly, sweeping, peeling potatoes, making stock, sweeping again.

When dusk fell, the men were still not returned. We built up the fire and sat waiting.

Marie had just said, 'I wonder how drunk he will be,' when we heard the sound of men singing.

Father's face was alight, his eyes dancing. 'We have offered to match anything the sheep farmers will pay. Colquhoun assures us we shall be successful.'

He took Mother in his arms and they danced a jig around the room. Soon it was Marie's turn, then mine. Father was hugging and kissing us all and I do not remember being so happy before or since. My parents, giggling, went to bed early.

Marie put her ear to their door, came back smiling. She whispered, 'You'll not be the bairn of the house for much longer, Maggie.'

Yet six months later Mother's belly was as flat as the day Father came home singing.

At Whitsunday, we heard that sheriff's constables were approaching. The Erran was in spate from the meltings so they had to cross by the bridge. There the women gathered, with our menfolk behind warming themselves by a peat fire. I was sent to stand by the fire too, for the day was indeed bitter.

The sheriff was accompanied by our minister, Mister Buchanan, who looked as if he wished he were elsewhere. The women moved forward to meet them but Father and the other men fell to muttering among themselves, every now and then scowling at the business on the bridge.

'*Failte!*' Mother said to the sheriff, but she was not smiling. 'I'm thinking you are here on the laird's business. May we ask what business that is?'

The sheriff did not smile either. 'I think you know well enough.' He put one stout leg on the bridge but our women barred his way.

Minister Buchanan stepped forward. 'I beg you, ladies, let the officers pass.'

Mother looked sorry for him. 'Mister Buchanan,' she said, in the voice she used for chastising me. 'You have no place in such company.'

'I'm sure the laird won't turn you out,' said the sheriff, in a poor attempt at Gaelic. 'I'll do all I can to help if only you'll accept the warrants.' His tone was wheedling, like the men Mother warned me about.

'And what if you're wrong?' Mother pointed towards the Erran. 'Shall I lay myself and my bairns in that and be done with it?'

'Father, do something!' I hissed, but he turned his eyes away and stared, head bowed, at the grass beneath him.

The sheriff muttered to the minister and they made another attempt to cross. Minister Buchanan was allowed to continue but some younger women, including Marie, grabbed the sheriff's arms.

'Shall we throw you in, brave sheriff? Let's see how pretty you can swim.'

His face grew purple. 'Deliver the warrants!' he ordered his constables, who stepped onto the bridge, eyes darting all ways.

At first, Marie and her friends drew aside but then they mobbed them. 'Oh there's a handsome Seamais,' they cried, caressing the constables' cheeks then setting the warrants alight with burning peat.

The officers fled to their horses, with the sheriff stumbling behind.

'Why did my father say nothing?' I asked Mother afterwards.

Her lips were trembling and she kept dabbing at her eyes. Her voice shook. 'He cannot accept that his precious chief has betrayed us.'

Just like Grandfather's day, I thought. Father was still sulking by the fire. I grabbed him, shook him. 'It is a coward you are,' I said, 'to let my mother do the man's work today.'

His face grew as black as the clouds overhead and he struck me hard across the cheek. I winced but forced the tears away.

'You are your mother's daughter all right,' he cried. 'Spawn of cattle thieves and murderers.'

Mother lifted her head high, pulled me to her. 'At least MacGregors don't hide behind women,' she spat. 'Nor strike them.'

Father slept with the cattle for many a night afterwards.

The laird died and his son invited the tacksmen to a meeting. They rode off on a day of glorious sunshine, believing their offer had at last been accepted, but returned under louring skies like men about to be hanged.

Father was weeping. 'We held out our hands for new leases and were handed eviction warrants instead.'

'It's a pity there were no women to save you,' Mother snapped, then ran outside into driving rain.

The clearances began in the upper strath. We watched silently as ninety-seven people left their homes, meeker than the sheep that would replace them. With nowhere to go, they camped under a tarpaulin behind the tiny church. Mercifully, the weather was warm, for all they had to protect them were horse cloths and plaids.

A soft-spoken stranger was at the church. Minister Buchanan said he was from the London *Times*.

My father sniffed loudly. 'Newspapers will not feed them.'

A week later, the churchyard was bare except for the graves.

Two years passed. No sheriff's constables came. It seemed the London *Times* had influence after all but when our blackest hour arrived they sent nobody north to witness it. The new war with Russia had captured the news.

At seven o'clock on a dark morning, the last of March, we heard whistling from our watchers on the braeside.

'Are you ready?' said Mother, wrapping her shawl around her neck.

Father glowered by the door. 'I'll not be coming with you, Beth,' he said.

'I'm begging you, John. Think of your daughters.'

Father shook his head. 'The sheriff will not hurt women, Beth.'

'You coward.' Mother spat at his feet.

Father grabbed Mother's wrists. 'I'm no coward,' he said, his voice breaking. 'If there was an army to fight, I'd fight it. But you can't fight pieces of paper. You've turned the sheriff away before and no doubt you'll turn him now, but we're finished in Stratherran and you know it.'

Mother shook herself free. 'You're no husband of mine,' she said.

We'd marched four miles down the glen before we saw the sheriff and his constables. We drew our shawls over our heads and waited as they emerged from a wood.

The sheriff shouted, using his bad Gaelic, 'Stand aside. You are blocking the Queen's highway.'

We stood our ground and he took out the Riot Act, but we felt bold. We were about eighty strong, including perhaps a dozen men, outnumbering the sheriff's force by two to one.

He returned the paper to his pocket and turned to his constables. 'Clear the way,' he shouted, this time in English.

We parted our ranks to let our men through but most were already scurrying back to Stratherran. The police slow-marched towards us, chanting an obscene verse in Scots. When they were close enough for us to see Queen Victoria's insignia, Mother read them a letter from the factor, Colquhoun, in which he denied authorising evictions. Two constables laughed in her face and one struck her down. My cries echoed hers as they beat her about the head with their batons. She rolled over, groaning, shielding herself with her arms but they kicked them aside and drew their nailed boots across her face, chest, and shoulders.

I felt the blood power through my veins. 'That's my mother, you murderers,' I screamed, rushing at them, pounding them with my bare fists, clawing their faces.

'Och, a wee hellcat is it?' sneered a foul-breathed hero, grabbing my waist.

He struck me on my head but someone pulled him back and I staggered into a field and plunged into a bush. He parted the branches, raining baton blows on my head until I crawled out and crouched at his feet. He was not done with me yet. Pushing me over, he pressed his baton across my breasts, kneeling with all his weight on it while he clamped handcuffs to my wrists. Oh the pain of it! I was squealing and fighting for breath at the same time.

'You Hieland bitch,' he swore, and worse besides. He got up at last, gave me a parting kick and left me on the ground.

I watched as the police charged into the rest of our women, who were trying to flee up the brae. They flailed without mercy, even the pregnant, the old, and the frail.

'Sweet Jesus! No!' I shrieked as Marie fell. I tried to reach her but was kicked down again, forced to watch her lying senseless on the freshly ploughed earth.

Dogs appeared and soon were everywhere, licking the blood that now lay in pools on the road and stained the grass and the soil. Two men started kicking Marie and I saw her scalp ripped away by their hobnails. Huge hanks of her long dark hair, clotted with blood, were scattered over the ground.

'That's for Whitsunday on the bridge,' one of the men said.

People arrived, riding and running – Father, the minister and other valiant men of our township.

'Dear God in heaven!' cried Minister Buchanan. He struck the sheriff across the face. 'How dare you attack defenceless women.'

Father stood, mouth open, horror distorting his face. He knelt down, cradled Mother. 'Oh, my Beth,' he said. 'I never dreamed this could happen.' He looked over towards me. 'I'm sorry, Maggie. I'm sorry. Believe me, if I had known…'

I could not bear to look at him.

At least twenty women and girls lay on the ground.

One man alone, a seventy-year-old Waterloo veteran, had fought beside us. Blood-soaked, he sat in tears. 'I never saw the Frenchies treated so badly as our poor women,' he said.

Minister Buchanan approached. His face was dark. He knelt beside me, put his arms around me. He said Marie was dead.

Mother and I were arrested as ringleaders. Since hearing of Marie's death, Mother had turned into a babbling idiot.

'For God's sake, pity the woman,' Minister Buchanan said to the sheriff.

The sheriff sneered at him. 'You should have asked that before raising your hand to me.'

We were roped to horse rings outside the factor's house and made to stand for hours in nothing but our shifts. While we shivered and bled and grieved, the sheriff was indoors drinking whisky.

When he finally left the factor's house, he laughed. 'You should have come in out of the cold,' he said. Then he had us dragged in chains to the tollbooth.

I had a visitor that night. He stank of stale sweat and sour whisky and I recognised him as the coward who had beaten me so savagely.

'I haven't finished with you yet, my darling,' he leered then dragged me upstairs to a small guardroom and threw me onto a straw palliasse. I felt nothing and cared even less as he lumped himself on top of me. It was as if I was already dead. Like Marie.

On our second night, the door was unlocked again and Mother began to whimper.

In came Minister Buchanan. 'You may go home,' he said.

But our homes were ours no longer and Marie was already buried. Father led us to her grave and there fell to his knees, kissed the dark soil and wept as I had never seen anyone weep before.

Mother suddenly found her voice. 'Oh, John, John,' she said softly, stroking Father's black hair.

I left them, grieved quietly on my own.

I could scarcely believe it when the laird's men came recruiting. 'We need troops for Crimea. Who will fight for their country?'

For once, Father spoke up. 'We have no country,' he said. 'Let the sheep fight the Russians.'

I was almost proud of him then.

A week later, wagons arrived to carry us to the tall ships. As my parents stood in line, I slipped away into the heather. A piper began to play 'Stratherran no more' and our people stood bareheaded, heads bowed. The laird's men moved towards them but suddenly stopped, took off their bonnets, waited silently until the lament was done.

And today they are burning our homes.

Power to the Lonely

Agnes Makepeace taps a foot on her hallway floor, glares at the man who is blocking her front doorway.

He waves a bunch of papers. 'Your home is historic,' he says. 'A B2 aluminium prefab. We want to put it on the heritage list.'

His eyes are all lit up and there's what Agnes considers a funny look on the face beneath. She doesn't like people giving her funny looks. In her experience, they lead to things that aren't funny at all. 'Historic?' she says. 'It's hardly older than what I am.' She shuts the door on him, counts to ten then moves to her sitting room, looks out of a window.

The man has retreated to the pavement. He's scratching his head, looking back at the house, at the snatch of weedy lawn in front of it.

'Calling me historic,' Agnes mutters, then a hard knot of resistance rises in her, compels her to open the window. 'Leave me alone,' she shouts at the man. 'I don't need no list.' Her words snag her throat. She coughs hard but the obstruction remains.

The man shakes his head, writes something on his papers, heads for a car parked across the road, drives off.

For several minutes, Agnes watches the space where the car stood, then she coughs again and this time her throat clears. She closes her window, gazes around her living room, taking in its thread-worn Axminster, the cheap prints lining its walls, the utility furniture that has been there a few years longer than she has. 'Since your dad was in Monty's army getting himself killed,' her mother used to say, then would invariably have to wipe a tear away.

'Bugger historic,' Agnes says and feels the need to wipe her own eyes. As she does, there's a sudden croaking from the cuckoo in an old Black Forest clock above her mantelpiece. 'Blimey, girl,' she mutters as she registers the time, 'better get a move on.'

She slips a bottle-green coverall over the beige jumper and slacks she has worn all day then repairs her face quickly in front of the bathroom mirror, forces a comb through her grey frizzy hair. 'You'll have to do,' she tells her reflection.

She leaves barely in time to catch the seven minutes past five bus at the stop down her road. She calls it 'going for the tram'.

Her mother used to say that on the nights she went out boozing, I'm just going for the tram, Agnes. I might be late back. One such night in 1971, a rainy one, her mother was permanently late back. She ran across the road at chucking-out time, slipped on wet rails, and was killed by the tram that should have borne her safely home. Two weeks later, the trams stopped forever but in Agnes's head they keep on running.

The bus deposits Agnes on the wrong side of a throbbing urban dual carriageway. There's an underpass ten yards away but she won't go down there, no fear. Last time she did, a wino felt her bum. Agnes can smell piss and worse wafting up from the void beyond the underpass steps. She scurries past, eyes steering straight ahead then waits at the kerb, seeking a gap in the rush-hour traffic. The first leg of her run is accompanied by frenzied hoots from home-going workers in fast-as-spit cars but Agnes makes the central reservation intact. She catches her breath before taking on the other carriageway (city-bound so less frenetic) to reach the office block where she's contracted to labour at five-thirty.

With her shift-mate Carol, a barrel of a woman with gigantic drooping bosoms, Agnes gathers waste-paper bins in a long, open-plan office on the sixth floor and empties them into plastic bags. They stack the latter outside the lifts in the central core, ready to go down to the garbage truck. That done, she and Carol fire up squat vacuum cleaners and run them over the beige and dog poo carpet squares between the desks.

Some office people are still working. Agnes smiles as she spies a balding man she imagines must be close to redundancy, which someone told her is the new word for retirement. His name's Billy and he reminds her of Sid James, of television evenings in the common room, before they closed the Mount.

She aims her vacuum cleaner in a direction that will bring her obliquely to Billy's desk. She doesn't want to approach directly because that would look as if she was being forward, and nice girls aren't like that. As she skirts the windows overlooking the dual carriageway, she notices one of the tramps from the underpass entering a small garden laid out on the site of an old warehouse. It's walled on the three sides that don't abut the road. The tramp moves towards the rear left-hand corner. He looks shifty. Like they all do, thinks Agnes, as he scans over his shoulder then turns so his back faces the corner. He drops his trousers and squats with his ragged overcoat hoisted over his haunches.

Agnes claps a hand to her mouth. 'Crikey,' she squeals.

Billy strains forward to peer out of the window. Carol lollops over, bosoms swinging like lead-weighted, half-deflated balloons.

'He doesn't think anyone can see him,' says Billy, fingering his chin. 'He looks all around but never up.'

'Too used to looking at life in the gutter, I suppose,' says Carol.

Agnes stares at her, mouth agape. 'Blimey,' she says.

'Blimey what?'

'You're talking like one of them bastards.'

'Which bastards, Aggie?' Carol has one eye cocked, winks at Billy from the other one.

'The ones what ask the questions. Then stick wires on you when you don't know the answers.'

Billy squints at Carol. She shrugs then shakes her head. Billy rolls his eyes.

The tramp hoists his trousers, smoothes his coat over his flanks and waddles to a wooden bench.

'Poor bugger's got no paper,' Agnes says. She clenches her teeth then steers her vacuum cleaner across the carpet tiles, missing more than she hits. She retrieves her bag from her locker, secretes herself in a cubicle in the ladies'.

Five minutes later, Carol comes in. 'You all right, Aggie?' she calls.

Agnes grunts a reply, flushes clean water down the pan.

When Agnes leaves for home, the tramp is still on the bench, spread out so he covers the entire seating space.

The traffic is light now and Agnes crosses the road without hindrance.

'Here,' she says to the tramp, waving a pack of toilet tissues she removed from the janitor's stock.

The tramp gapes at her then his eyes roll slowly upwards to the giant building on the other side of the road. Through the matted fuzz and dirt on his face, Agnes sees the slow beginnings of embarrassment.

'It's all right,' she says. 'It was only me what saw.'

The tramp takes to waving at Agnes whenever their paths cross. One evening, he whips a bunch of flowers from behind his back and, bowing so low Agnes expects his spine to crack, offers them to her.

Fighting an impulse to ask where he'd pinched them from, she performs a version of a curtsey she saw some posh cow do on the telly. Her cheeks boil.

The tramp is smiling. It's only now Agnes realises that she can actually see his face.

'You've had a shave,' she says, gobsmacked. She wonders where he keeps a razor.

Did he blush? Agnes isn't sure but the question's forgotten as she peers more closely at the tramp's features.

'Hey,' she says. 'Didn't you use to be at the Mount?'

The tramp reacts by moving back a pace and hunching, head down, as if trying to disappear inside himself.

'It's all right,' Agnes says, her voice softening. 'They can't hurt you now.'

The tramp's head moves halfway to upright. Watery blue eyes regard Agnes's, flinching now and then. When he speaks, it is slow, with a hint of stutter. 'I...had to get out,' he says.

'Yeah,' says Agnes. 'We all did. They shut the bloody place down.'

The tramp slowly raises his head all the way. His back straightens too, and this time Agnes does hear it crack.

'You need oilin',' she says and the tramp grins.

He extends his left arm and she stares at it momentarily then links her right arm with it. They stroll together along the street, away from the underpass. He leads her to the park.

Agnes pulls him up in front of the gates. ''Ere, what are you up to?' she says, screwing up her face as she glares at his.

'Cup of tea,' the tramp says. 'No harm in that.'

The stutter has gone and the voice sounds posh to Agnes now. She finds something else she didn't expect, in his watery stare.

'You wasn't one of us, you was one of them, wasn't you?' she says, shaking her head. 'You're a bleedin' doctor.'

'Was,' the tramp says. 'So is tea all right, then?'

Agnes tries to nod while she's still shaking her head. 'Go on then,' she says.

The tramp makes his way to a mobile booth by the main pathway. Agnes waits on a bench, gazes at a duck pond, her face contorting as she wrestles with the new facts filling her head.

The tramp returns with two plastic cups and biscuits in a vacuum pack. 'I forgot to ask if you take milk and sugar.'

'What's in the ones you got?'

'Milk and sugar.'

'Then that's what I take.' Agnes smiles at him and he smiles back. She notices he has a front tooth missing.

The light begins to fade and the tramp peers at the clock on the façade of the big house that sits in the middle of the park. 'They'll be locking the gates in ten minutes,' he says. 'I'd better see you to your bus.'

Agnes scratches her nose. 'Where will you go after that?'

'Probably back here.'

'But the gates'll be locked.'

The tramp shrugs. 'Won't stop me.'

Agnes inclines her head to one side, squints up at him. 'Where d'you kip, then? Under a bush?'

'Depends. The best place is the bowls pavilion. I have a colleague who can pick the lock but he might not be around tonight. That's why it depends.'

Agnes thinks for a moment. 'Don't seem right,' she says, 'a doc kipping in a shed. No, you're coming home with me. No funny business, though. I gotta couch you can use. A bath wouldn't go amiss neither.'

Twenty minutes later, they walk into the street where Agnes lives.

''Ere we are then,' she says as she inserts her key in her navy-blue door.

Somewhere between teatime and bedtime, Agnes and the tramp trade names. His, she learns, is Arthur. Something makes her tell him about the man who called her home historic.

Arthur nods. 'I expect he was from English Heritage. They keep lists of special buildings. To make sure nobody knocks them down.'

'Special buildings?' Agnes is frowning. 'You mean my house is special?'

She recalls the school she attended being called special too, although it never looked anything much to her. Whenever she asked why she couldn't go to the one all the other kids went to, her mother said, You have special needs, Agnes, and those kids are just ordinary. It didn't stop them pointing fingers at her and jeering.

'Reckon so,' Arthur says. 'Only a few of these left now.' He waves a hand at Agnes's walls, her ceiling. 'You could in fact claim that it's extra special, a palace no less. The very first tenants called them that: little palaces. They were so impressed with having central heating, a fitted kitchen, a refrigerator, and a proper bathroom.'

Agnes is nodding twenty to a dozen. Her eyes are aglow. 'Do you know, Arthur,' she says, 'you're exactly right. "My little tin palace." That's what my mum always called this house.'

'There you are then, Agnes,' Arthur says. He thumbs his chin. 'The Heritage man's sure to come back, you know.'

He beams at Agnes and she thinks that being special isn't so bad after all.

'Well, when he does, I'll say it's all right to put it on his list,' she says. 'Just as long as he don't call me historic.'

In the morning, Agnes places a cup of tea and a plate of over-buttered toast beside Arthur. He is prone, eyes shut, on her sofa.

'Wakey, wakey,' she coos.

Arthur's eyes open. They look startled as they focus on the flowery yellow pyjamas Agnes gave him to wear. He pats them as if to make sure they really exist.

'We'd better get you some clothes,' Agnes says. 'I've chucked yours in the bin.'

She takes a cloth tape from a battered Quality Street tin, measures Arthur's chest, waist, inside leg (gets him to hold the crotch end), neck and feet. 'We won't bother with your head,' she says. 'Nobody wears hats no more.'

She leaves Arthur sipping tea and takes a bus downtown. None of your cheapo shops, she decides, not for a doctor, but her jaw drops when she sees the big stores' prices. 'They want you to buy the flipping shop as well,' she says to anyone in earshot. She buys underpants and socks on special offer then switches downmarket, visits the stall where she buys most of her own clothes.

'Hey, Lil,' she says to its ruddy-faced owner, a roly-poly woman of indeterminable age. 'Lookin' for something decent for me brother. Not seconds. Large size. No foreign muck.'

'No foreign muck?' says Lil. 'You having a laugh or something?' She rummages in plastic bins, offers Agnes corduroy slacks, a white shirt in a cellophane pack, and an acrylic jumper in a tweedy mix. 'Made in China,' Lil says. 'Twenty per cent off for cash.'

In a charity shop's window, Agnes spots a gentleman's dinner jacket and trousers. She almost presses her nose through the glass, picturing Arthur wearing them to some evening do at a swish hotel. She imagines being the woman on his arm, all dolled up in a magenta gown.

The shop manager discourages her from buying the dinner jacket. 'Here's a lovely lounge suit,' he says. 'Far more practical, and it's Savile Row, absolute top quality. Should fit your brother. And how about this sports jacket? Pure new wool, Donegal tweed.'

Agnes rolls Savile Row and Donegal Tweed round her tongue, finds them fitting for a doc. She leaves with the suit and jacket plus an overcoat in wool and cashmere, extra large to allow a bit more room. After she's paid, she spots a pair of black brogues that have a shine you could dazzle yourself with if you weren't careful. She checks them: just Arthur's size. Then she looks in her purse, finds it wanting.

'Tell you what, love,' the manager says. 'I'll throw them in too.'

'I don't want no charity,' Agnes says, her face clouding.

'No, no, love, it's a discount. You've made a bulk purchase. I forgot to knock it off when I was doing the bill.'

Agnes studies the manager's eyes. When he doesn't blink, she says, 'Well, all right then, if you say so. As long as it ain't charity. I pay me own way, I do.'

Arthur's eyes flood. 'Why,' he says, 'are you being so good to me?' He strokes the suit and overcoat. 'Agnes, these must have been frightfully expensive.'

Agnes grins. 'Fell off a lorry, didn't they? Right, Arthur, let's see what you're like dressed up.' She points to a door. 'Use that room. I'll put the kettle on.'

She makes two mugs of tea and puts them on a tray, carries it into the living room and almost drops it. Arthur is standing by the mantelpiece. He's wearing the suit and the brogues. He looks smashing, she thinks.

'You're a real gent,' Agnes says. She almost said 'prince'.

Arthur performs a little bow.

'Need to get you a tie, though,' Agnes says.

At ten to five, Agnes takes her coverall from its hook. 'Got to go for the tram, Arthur,' she says. 'Back at ten past seven. Don't go away.'

At work, she swishes her feather duster, disturbing almost nothing. She gazes over to where Billy sits. His tie's slack and the top buttons of his shirt are open. She can see sweat stains under his arms. She can do better than Billy.

As Agnes gets home, the bells of St Margaret's, four streets away, strike the hour. She decides that she'll make a nice stew tonight.

'I'm back,' she calls as she steps into her living room.

But Arthur is not in it, or the kitchen, the bathroom, or either bedroom, because all the doors are open and Agnes can see the emptiness. He's taken the overcoat, but left the tweed jacket, the corduroys, everything he wasn't wearing when she left for work.

'Well, that's very nice,' Agnes says. 'I don't know...' She feels a hardness starting in her throat.

She sits in the kitchen, watching the clock on the wall, doesn't feel like making stew any more.

Agnes's pulse quickens as she hears footsteps outside but it's only her neighbour, off to feed the pokies at the pub. She scans her street; no people, only a yellow car – a taxi, it looks like, turning into the road.

She shrugs, goes back indoors then, moments later, hears a timid knock on her front door, as if a sparrow's requesting entrance.

It's Arthur, holding a package wrapped in newspaper. 'Thought I'd treat you,' he says. 'Sorry I'm late, Agnes, there was a bit of a queue.'

Agnes takes Arthur's package into the kitchen. It contains two battered fish and a mountain of chips.

'I'll warm these up,' she shouts into the living room. 'You come and put the kettle on.' She feels as if a sunbeam has broken free and come down to lighten her life.

The evening is clear, the air gentle. Agnes parades Arthur along the sort of streets where office people or even doctors might live. They turn an unexpected corner.

Agnes's feet stutter to a halt. She recognises a pair of gateposts, each inscribed with two words etched in her mind as well as in this stone. Huge wrought iron gates span the gap between the posts.

'The Mount,' Agnes says in a voice that comes out like sandpaper. Her arms reach out, cling to Arthur.

Then she realises that, although its guardian walls still stand, gaunt and grey, she can't see the building itself. She breathes a little easier, peers through the gates.

The building is indeed gone. Excavators, dumper trucks, and portacabins squat on its site.

'So the Mount wasn't special,' Agnes says, frowning. 'They didn't want that on no list.'

'No,' Arthur says. 'It wasn't special.' He is gazing at Agnes with an unhappy stare. His eyes fill. 'There was a girl...' he says. 'She died.'

'I know. Jeanie Treadwell.'

'It was my fault... I...miscalculated.' Beads of sweat roll down Arthur's face.

'Was you struck off?'

'Might have been better if I had been.' Arthur's voice breaks at 'had been' and he starts sobbing.

Agnes pats his head as he leans it against her. 'There, there now,' she says. 'You don't have to worry about nothing no more.' Who'd have thought it? she thinks, I'm the doctor now and Arthur's the one with special needs.

She notices a signboard a few metres inside the gateway. It is headed EXECUTIVE HOMES FOR SALE but the remaining detail is obscured because someone has sprayed POWER TO THE LONELY over it in large black scrawls.

'Homes,' she snorts. 'You can't build homes with bricks and mortar. And you can't buy them neither.'

Arthur straightens himself, stops crying. As quick as his tears began, his face creases into a smile. 'You mean builders can only make a house, and it needs people living in it, their love, laughter, sadness, tears to turn it into a home?'

Agnes nods. Her face feels as if it's caught the sun. 'Arthur,' she says, 'our house could be home, couldn't it?'

'It could,' he says then hesitates. 'Does that mean...?'

Agnes nods again. 'Our own little palace,' she says.

Arthur squeezes her hand, takes her arm.

As they move on, Agnes casts a final look at the Mount, rereads the graffiti on the developer's board. 'Power to the lonely,' she mouths, finds the words fitting.

For a Yellow Jersey

I know about riding up mountains. And down again. I have earned the right to make that claim. Tomorrow I shall start my tenth Tour de France. It will be my last race of any kind. My swan song. It is the ideal occasion for this – a spectacle seen by millions the world over, even those who normally never watch a bike race. A place on the podium in Paris would be my perfect result – if I fail, it will not be for want of trying. Then I swear I shall hang up my wheels for good. A succession of dismal comebacks is not for me. I want people to remember my good years. I have no wish to see their embarrassment – or worse, pity – as a faded has-been makes a bloody fool of himself.

During a lifetime, there are days when everything will go just right. But you must learn to recognise them. They are the times when you may – no, *must* – seize the moment without fear of the consequences. Because, believe me, on such days success is for the taking; it just depends upon how hungry you are.

I am a peasant from the Limousin; I was born hungry. But I've had my luck also. I have won classics – Paris–Roubaix, Milan–San Remo, and big stage races – the Giro d'Italia once and the Vuelta à España twice. But the biggest prize of all, the Tour de France, La Grande Boucle, has always eluded me. Fourth place once, and twice King of the Mountains – that is all I have achieved in nine attempts. The Tour has sucked me up, drained me, bloodied me, and literally spat me out in pieces, yet each year I've come back for more. There's something about the Tour that does that to you. That's what Inga doesn't understand.

You might think that's ironic, because it was in the Tour that I met her. Three years ago. I fell in love with her name before I ever saw Inga herself. I was reading the race reports, and (it was in *La Gazzetta dello*

Sport) one writer's name stood out. Inga Storm Torstensen. The name evoked so many images, delightful and disturbing, that it kept running through my mind all night. I finally met its owner on the Champs Elysées, where I won the final stage of that year's race. I'd suffered the indignity of giving my blood and peeing for the dope control and looked forward to a relaxing bath and my first full night's sleep after nearly four weeks' racing. I saw this blonde vision striding purposefully towards me. At first I thought she was a fan – yes, cycling has its groupies too. Then I noticed the Press badge on the pocket of her blue cotton shirt.

'Monsieur Montignac? Could you please give me an interview?'

Could I? Oh, I certainly could, especially when I learned she was the name of my dreams made flesh. She said I was lucky to meet her, and I truly believed I was. But she meant that she was standing in for a colleague and didn't normally cover the Tour. So maybe I was lucky twice over. We drank beer together into the small hours of the morning, then she insisted on driving me to Ghent, where I was booked to ride a criterium. Suffering from a giant hangover, I packed on the fifteenth lap.

In the following weeks, Inga, claiming she wanted a fly-on-the-wall view of a bike-rider's life, ferried me around Belgium and France while I completed my post-Tour contracts.

That year, the world championships were held near Inga's home in Aosta. She asked, as we seemed to get on together, would I like to stay with her? Saying yes brought two more of those days on which everything runs perfectly. I won my rainbow jersey on the first, and married my beautiful Viking on the second.

Last season, my first as a married man, was a disaster. No wins, just three lousy places in the first six. I told myself that the riders who beat me were probably on EPO. So they might have been, but that had never stopped me from winning before. No, I failed because I had lost that vital hunger – the inborn need to win. Maybe marriage made me soft, for I had to bully myself into going out training. Or maybe I believed in the curse of a world champion's jersey. For only the second time in my career, I failed to finish the Tour. It was such a stupid thing, though predictable,

I suppose. So anxious was I to do justice to the rainbow jersey on my back that I descended the Izoard far too fast, misjudged a hairpin, and sailed over the edge. My thoughts at that moment are still too difficult to put down. Let's just say I thought I was destined for the big chain gang in the sky. I came to earth with one hell of a bump, all tangled up in my bike. My right arm was sticking out at an unusual angle. I didn't feel anything at first, then pain began to filter through the shock, increasing with such intensity that soon my brain could cope no more and I lost consciousness. I was vaguely aware of a steady chop-chop-chop that must have been the helicopter lifting me off the mountainside, but the next thing I truly remember is waking up in a hospital bed, with Inga sitting by my side white with anxiety. She'd watched the accident on *Eurosport* and said she almost passed out herself.

Luckily my head stayed in one piece, but I'd broken my right arm, right leg, collarbone, and several ribs. I spent the next three months as a training course for bone doctors.

Inga and I had already agreed that I would ride for one more season but now she pleaded, 'Give up now, Eddy. Don't leave it another year.'

But I did not listen; oddly enough, the accident had brought back my will to win. That season may have been over for me, but I was looking forward eagerly to the next. Inga accepted it in the end. Or at least I thought she did.

Eventually I began to get about – on crutches first, then a walking stick. Then came the glorious day when I was allowed out on the bike. Low gears, gentle pace. No hills. My muscles regained bulk and as my fitness returned I began to train in earnest, much to Inga's dismay.

Winter came on and in January we went to Courchevel. Inga is wonderful to watch on the slopes. Her graceful twists and turns and the triumphant little wiggle she gives at the end of a good run are worthy of a ballerina. Five years ago, she won the world downhill championship. That brought her the job with *La Gazzetta*, and she spends most of her winter reporting the big skiing events.

Like many pro cyclists, I love to ski. My *soigneur* says the two sports use the same muscle groups. Be that as it may, I've never been more than an average skier and can never hope to match Inga on the slopes. But, fool that I am, I did try. Maybe I was just testing my fitness, or maybe I was trying to impress her. Whatever the reason, I took what she told me was a most impressive tumble, and my reward was a broken ankle. Back in plaster again.

I missed Paris–Nice and all the early classics. To crown my disappointment, the Hirondelle team boss, Antonin Lefarge, left me out of the Tour de France team.

Putain de merde! I fumed. I wept. I ranted. I threatened.

Tonin was unmoved. 'Look, Eddy,' he said, as if addressing a baby, 'it's your last season. Take it easy – you have some lucrative contracts. Just smile for the cameras and pocket the money.'

But I wanted to go out in a rush of glory. The world must remember that I finished at the top.

Inga made all the right sympathetic noises, but could not hide the look of relief on her face. However, stubborn peasant that I am, I ignored her concern and Tonin's disloyalty and continued to train hard every day, putting in perhaps two hundred kilometres in the hills around Saint-Etienne, where the Hirondelle team is based. I prayed for a miracle.

It happened when Jean-Luc Bardinet wrote off his car and his legs one evening as he drove from Lyon to his home in La Rochelle. It wasn't the sort of miracle I'd wanted – Jean-Luc is a nice guy and now it seems he might never ride again.

Tonin didn't exactly beg me to take his place but came very close. There was only one drawback – I must ride for Claudio Corelli. Tonin had signed the Italian during the close season, seeing in him the potential Tour winner I had long ceased to be. Corelli may soar up the mountain passes like an eagle, but he's a tortoise when he descends them. My climbing is less spectacular but I'm rarely out of the first half-dozen over the cols. My speciality, despite my disastrous crash last year, is hurtling down them faster than anyone else. Tonin's idea was that I would stay with Corelli on the climbs, show him the way down then tow him to the finish, where I would pull aside and watch him take the victory.

I was furious, but kept my mouth shut because I had to have that ride. On the road, events might turn out to be very different. 'Renard', the cognoscenti call me, not because I smell like a fox, but because I know instinctively when, where and how to make a winning move. The trouble is I earned the name when I still had the speed and strength to burn the opposition off my wheel.

Inga was furious with Tonin too, though for a different reason. She shook me by the shoulders. 'Eddy, last year was a warning. Courchevel was too. Promise me you won't ride. You're too old. Don't make me a widow before I'm thirty.'

'For heaven's sake, Inga, I'm only thirty-three. Poulidor came third at forty. And more than one rider has been my age when he first won the Tour.'

She became very quiet, hardly spoke to me for three days. Then she issued her ultimatum: 'Eddy, I've decided – it's either the Tour or me. I can't go through last year again.'

She could be bluffing, I thought. But if not, I might still have a second chance with her, whereas the Tour won't wait for me. 'Inga, you don't understand,' I said. 'I have to ride one last time. If you can't allow me that, then I'm sorry…'

We have been racing for nearly three weeks now. From Bayeux, we snaked across Normandy and Brittany, and down through the Bordeaux country to the Pyrénées. Predictably, the sprinters shone in the flat stages, men like Jurgens. But they become shadows of themselves in the mountains. The chief danger comes from automatons like Frantz, who has held the yellow jersey since the last time-trial on the flat stages. Riders like him sit in over the cols, letting the climbers pace them. They know that once out of the mountains they can take many minutes out of their rivals over a piddling thirty-odd kilometre time-trial. For me, men like these kill the Tour while the real heroes sweat their balls off to bring the drama that the crowds come to see. Frantz and his ilk rely on their heart-rate monitors, and ration out their energy with almost clinical precision. I do not fear them because the moment their electronic regulators bleep in alarm, they will ease back, and that is when they can be beaten. If you really want to win, that is the time to dig down to your deepest resources and force your body to work even harder.

Obeying Lefarge's orders, I shepherd Corelli across the Pyrénées. Over the Aubisque, where bone-chilling rain drives across the bare mountain and pierces our suffering bodies. Over the gaunt, grey Tourmalet, where we can hardly see the road in front of us through the mist and constant, freezing drizzle. Up the green zigzagging snake of the Peyresourde beneath a raging sun that saps our strength. Our sweat leaves salt crusts on our sun-browned skin and we would cheerfully kill for shade and water.

Despite all our efforts, Frantz leaves the Pyrénées in yellow. Corelli is second, at one minute forty-three seconds. I am in sixth place, five minutes down. It is a respectable position and, because they think I am past it, and only here as Corelli's lieutenant, the other pretenders ignore me.

We ride through the vineyards of Languedoc before turning north to Saint-Flour. The *domestiques* treat the stage as a holiday after the rigours of the mountains, and sample too much of the local vintage. Consequently, a greater number than usual relieve themselves straight from the saddle and the peloton becomes a dangerous place as riders try to avoid the unwelcome slipstream.

The stage from Saint-Flour to Clermont meanders along roads I train over each day and I use my local knowledge to pick up a few primes. Montbrison, where Inga and I rent a house, is only eighty kilometres away, so I contest the sprint at the stage finish, hoping that she will be there. I manage fourth place, but there is no sign of Inga. I telephone her, as I have done each day throughout the race. But, as I have come to expect, there is no reply. Inga is sticking to her decision. And I will stick to mine. I have to believe in myself again, so I concentrate my mind on tomorrow's time trial. This is a time trial with a difference: one I can do well in. Twelve kilometres up the Puy-de-Dome, scene of the epic struggle between Anquetil and Poulidor in 1964.

The day is warm and overcast, with little wind. Just how I like it. We set off at two-minute intervals in reverse order, with the *lanterne rouge* starting first, and the *maillot jaune*, Tony Frantz, last of all.

Remember what I said about recognising a perfect day? Well, right from the start I know this is going to be one. I do not have to think about what I am doing, my every action is automatic. I am at one with my bike. My tyres sing and my gears purr sweetly as I spin the pedals over the first six kilometres, a steady rise of one-in-fourteen. Then there is a kilometre of false flat before I pass through the tollgate and start the real climb. The mountain looks like an upturned ice cream cone with a road threading up it in a left-handed corkscrew.

On autopilot, I change down to 42 by 23 for the first section, a kilometre of one-in-seven. This is where I should start to suffer with each turn of the pedals. When this happens, your whole body protests, not just your legs. Breathing becomes a tremendous effort and your heart feels as if it will burst. But today when the pain barrier comes, I pass effortlessly beyond it onto another plane. The corkscrew becomes a little less steep, only one-in-eight now. Four kilometres left. I pass some riders, but I am concentrating too much to notice who or to count how many. They are not important. The crowds press together as I approach, then part at the last moment to let me through. My legs work in relentless, determined rhythm. I think of nothing other than getting my bike – my *vélo* – over the line in a shorter time than anyone else.

Chalked on the road ahead is Renard, *tu es le plus fort*. In spite of myself I smile. Today, I really believe I am the strongest. It spurs me on to go even faster, and soon the television mast is right ahead of me. I have crossed the finishing line. I do not feel tired, although I know I must be. All I feel is that intoxicating exhilaration that I experienced as a fourteen-year-old after my first ever race.

The waiting seems endless, but that means my time is good. Two minutes pass. No one in sight. Another minute – a blue and white jersey. It is one of the riders I passed on the way up. Over six minutes go by before Jimpy Delarousse, the rider who started two minutes behind me, crosses the line.

The eight-minute marker comes and goes. I have beaten Corelli! A rider is in view. It is Bobby Smith, an American, fourth overall. A further minute – two more riders in sight. I recognise the green and red of Corelli's Hirondelle jersey closely followed by Alain Rouillard in the blue white and red of the French national champion.

The ten-minute threshold passes. Jesus, I have won! I have beaten Tony bloody Frantz. So much for his heart monitor and so much for Tonin's confidence in me. I've almost forgotten what winning is like. It's the most wonderful feeling in the world. Better than sex. Most of the time.

I have to wait over three more minutes before a scowling Frantz appears. After all the calculations are done, I have moved up to third overall. I am satisfied. If I can hold on to that until Paris, I will have proved my point. Frantz still has the *maillot jaune*, but only by four seconds now, from Corelli. I am exactly two minutes behind Frantz, so one fifty-six adrift of Corelli. Rouillard, now in fourth place, is one thirty-nine behind me.

The press and TV go mad. Headlines scream, Renard is back. I am besieged by reporters, who shove microphones in my face. Oh, I love it all. I am grinning like a Paris cat. Lefarge looks sheepish but Corelli's face is impassive. Neither offers congratulations. I telephone Inga again. Still no reply.

In the next two stages, nobody with hopes of overall victory wants to attack. They are thinking of the Alps to come. In the first, we pass through Montbrison, but I look in vain for Inga's face amongst the crowd. The stage ends in a bunch sprint at Saint-Etienne, and Corelli and I stay at the back, protected by the entire Hirondelle team. On the following stage, to Chambéry, an unknown *domestique* is allowed to break away and win on his own by seventeen minutes.

That evening when I call, it is clear Inga has been home, because the answer phone switches in. It feels odd listening to my own recorded voice telling me I am unable to come to the phone. After the beep, I say, 'I love you, Inga.' She doesn't answer, but I am sure that she is listening.

The Tour bursts into life. The route from Chambéry to Montgenèvre takes in the Col d'Izoard, scene of my violent exit last year. It is 2,360 metres of awesome wilderness. Corelli, Frantz, Rouillard and I are in a leading group of perhaps a dozen riders. The climb starts innocently enough. We ride halfway up the slopes along two narrow valleys and pass the Brunissard ski resort before ascending a steep rack of hairpins to the vast lunar landscape of the *casse désert*. Tyres and spokes pop and ping as we thread cautiously through the stones littering the road, which is no more than a shelf hacked out of the scree slope. A great black cloud looms ominously above as we pass Coppi's memorial and round a right-hand bend towards the final zigzags. Corelli is watching me like a hawk and Frantz and Rouillard as usual are content to sit on our wheels. The rain starts as we cross the summit.

The fans gathered there offer us newspapers, which we shove down our jerseys as a defence against the cold and wet. The rain begins to bucket down as we start our descent. As we approach the first bend, I check the faces of the other riders. They look shit-scared.

'Come on,' I say to Corelli. 'We can lose this lot.'

I jump away immediately and Corelli has no option but to follow.

At the next hairpin, he baulks. 'No, Eddy, it's too dangerous. Stay back with me.'

I look behind. We have opened up a fifteen-second gap. 'Are you coming or not?' I hiss.

Corelli shakes his head.

'Well, fuck you then.'

I tear off down the hairpins like a man with a death wish. I hear a rider skid and fall off. Corelli and the others brake and crawl round the bend like Burgundy snails. I grit my teeth and go faster still, but still shiver as I pass the spot where I became airborne last July. This time however, my wheels stay on the road, and coming into Briançon I am one fifty up.

With eight kilometres left, I have gained another eight seconds, then my strength drains away suddenly, like water down a plughole. At five kilometres to go, I have only forty-seven seconds' advantage. The three-kilometre sign comes into view, and I hear the swish of tyres behind me. Dear God, don't let it be Frantz or Corelli. Two riders pass me as if I am standing still. One Italian and one Spaniard. Sod them.

Putting my head down, I press on, riding on willpower alone now. I daren't look behind to see where the others are. I cross the line in third place, exhausted, soaking wet, covered with filth from the road, and thoroughly pissed off. Corelli, Frantz and Rouillard arrive with the remains of their group thirty-one seconds later.

'Bastard.' Corelli spits on the ground in front of me.

I turn on him. I am in the mood for a fight. 'Don't you bastard me. You were told to follow me on the descents, but you just didn't have the bottle. If you'd stuck with me, you'd have the jersey now, so shut it.'

The stage result hasn't affected the pecking order. Frantz retains his four-second advantage over Corelli. I am still third but now only one twenty-nine behind Frantz.

Inga has switched the answer phone off. The phone just keeps on ringing.

Today is a 'gentle' stage over relatively minor cols. Yesterday's rain is still falling and we cocoon ourselves in waterproof jackets. The peloton is skittish and herds together nervously, giving an obscure Colombian rider the chance to slip away unnoticed and score a jubilant solo win.

Corelli and I still aren't speaking. Tonin gives us a pep talk, makes us shake hands before tomorrow's 227-kilometre leg round the valleys near Grenoble. This is the day we have all been dreading. The stage finishes on the summit of the Alpe d'Huez, the severest climb of all. I agree to help Corelli win the Tour there. I mean it too – if he really has what it takes.

After the climbs of the Cucheron and the Col du Coq, the race has split in two. The main peloton is ten minutes behind our group, which contains most of the leading contenders. We have to ride through a 400-metre long tunnel. It is unlit and very dark inside. I am riding at the front of the group and it is all very scary until we are safely round the bend in the middle and can at last see the chink of light at the tunnel's end. A clash of wheels behind, followed by the familiar sound of bikes and bodies hitting the road tells me that some riders failed to see the bend at all. But Corelli is safe with me. Emerging from the tunnel, we are momentarily blinded by the sudden change from dark to light. I note that Frantz and Rouillard have missed the crash too.

Plunging into a deep valley, we pass through a narrow gorge before reaching Bourg d'Oisans, a little place of steep roofs and deep eaves at the foot of Alpe d'Huez. It is a ghost town today, because its three thousand people are picnicking beside the ramps of road that zigzag up to the ski station. Thank goodness, the rain of the last two days is gone and the sun is shining. It is weather that suits me and I know I shall climb well.

From *virage* 20, each bend is numbered, so we always know exactly how many are left. A motley group, mainly Italians and Spaniards, edges away here, and within two kilometres two Italians, one a team-mate of Frantz, jump away on their own. When their lead has built up to one sixteen, I decide they've gone far enough. I give Corelli the eye and we shoot off in pursuit. Frantz immediately locks on to Corelli's wheel and Rouillard has to charge desperately after him.

We are joined by a couple of Spaniards and start to work together, except for Frantz and Rouillard, who refuse. At least Frantz has the excuse that his team mate is up ahead. Within a kilometre, we have recovered thirty seconds and soon absorb the breakaway, apart from the two Italians, who now have a lead of fifty-five seconds.

Yet another Italian shoots away and Frantz jumps after him too strongly, almost riding into the other's back wheel.

'Come on, Claudio,' I shout and drag Corelli up to them.

Frantz still won't do any work. Corelli begins to falter and slip back again.

I stay with him. 'You can't let Frantz escape. For fuck's sake, Claudio, dig in. Show the bastard your back wheel.'

Corelli's face is grey. He looks as if he is about to throw up. 'Eddy, I can't. I'm shagged out.'

I still don't make a move. I want no recriminations, no accusations of abandonment. 'Go on, Eddy,' he urges finally. 'Go on, before we both lose.'

I look round at the riders catching up with us, and ahead to the stocky figure of Frantz already disappearing round the next hairpin. I make my decision. '*Ciao*, Claudio.'

'*Ciao*, Eddy.' Corelli manages a rueful smile as I accelerate away.

Eleven kilometres to go. I have that feeling I had on the Puy de Dome. I am stepping lightly on the pedals, almost dancing, an angel of the mountains. Frantz and his Italian come into view. I draw them in and spit them out behind me as I dash past, too fast for Frantz to zap on to my wheel.

I dance on. If were to admit it, I would say that I am tired, I ache and my balls are numb from too many hours in the saddle. But I do not admit it. One of the two escapees appears in my sights and I aim carefully. He tries to grab my wheel as I pass, but today I am taking no passengers. I see the last Italian ahead. My head starts to swim as I slowly reel him in. He can't be more than ten seconds in front.

At last I reach the line of steep-pitched chalets and flat-roofed apartment blocks, and turn onto the level road of the ski station. Changing up to the 53 ring I force my legs to work that little bit harder. I almost have the Italian now but the banner is only metres away. I cross under it but don't know if I've caught him in time. My vision is hazy. I can't see him any more.

'Eddy! Eddy!'

I blink. I am on my back, blue sky above me. I lift my head and look down at myself. I am wrapped in a silver cloak and there are faces staring at me.

'Eddy, darling, you're all right. Oh, thank God!' It is Inga. She has come to see me after all.

They sit me in an ambulance for twenty minutes. 'You're fine,' declares the Tour doctor. 'You went into oxygen debt, that's all.'

'I was so scared when I saw you spread-eagled on the ground in that survival blanket,' Inga says. 'They were giving you oxygen, but the doctors assured me it was just a precaution.' She smiles. 'You have the yellow jersey. I'll see you in Paris.'

The *maillot jaune*? I'd forgotten the race. All I care about is that Inga is here.

It turns out that I lost the stage victory by five seconds. But, more importantly, Tony Frantz came in four fifty-one down. He must have blown up after I caught him. Claudio, who had looked like abandoning when I left him, finished a massive thirteen twenty-seven behind me and dropped to fifth overall. I am race leader by three twenty-two from Frantz. Tomorrow is a rest day, thank God. I need it, because, the following day, before the traditional procession into Paris, is the last day of real racing. A time trial over thirty-eight kilometres. Frantz will never take two minutes out of me over that distance, never mind the three minutes twenty-three seconds he needs to take the jersey back.

In any case, I have a notion that I can beat him. They say that wearing a yellow jersey is worth three seconds a kilometre. That makes one minute and fifty-four seconds. All things are possible.

But what the hell, there's a prize waiting for me in Paris anyway.

Dead Chrysanthemums

Don Fabio was a man permanently pleased with himself; you know the type – they wear pietistic smiles and their teeth are invariably capped. If he had been American, he would perhaps have been a politician but within his own fiefdom politics was confined to the dictionary. Don Fabio ruled. Absolutely.

He began life as plain Fabio, youngest of eight siblings in a fishing family. Being the only boy, he was held in adoration, so although his parents were poor, Fabio grew up expecting privilege. He believed his mother was a virgin and began to think she might even be a saint when, on her supplication, he was spared a fisherman's life.

'My son is destined for greatness, not drowning,' she told his father. Unlike his sisters, he escaped the gutting and cleaning of the catch too. 'That's women's work,' insisted his mother, so Fabio experienced the sea from the safety of dry land.

Alone on a headland above his village, he composed wild melodies that sang of turbulent water, treacherous winds, and naked rocks, teased them from his soul on uilleann pipes inherited from his maternal grandfather, a shipwrecked Irishman who never found his way back to Connemara.

To his sisters' embarrassment and his father's disgust, as Fabio neared puberty he took to dancing, ecstatic and often naked, on nights when the moon shone full. But his mother proclaimed, 'My son, the genius,' and Fabio's sanctimonious smile was set for life.

His panache in performing arts gained the attention of the local aristo, Don Paolo, who invited him to play at a summer soirée. As Fabio's chanters soared to their final shimmering wail, the audience sat in stolid silence.

Then the Don, who had appeared to be asleep, suddenly began to clap and cheer. Afterwards, he offered Fabio a non-musical career. 'You have a talent for surprise,' he said.

Fabio hummed and hawed but encouraged by the Don's nods said, 'I'll give it a month. Then if I don't like it...'

Don Paolo smiled in a way that Fabio found familiar but could not identify. He was unaware then that a Don Paolo request was one you didn't refuse. However, such callous ignorance was overlooked when Fabio proved he was adept at pressing more than Irish bellows into playing the tunes he wanted. He gleaned such golden pickings from the most dismal cases that Don Paolo said, 'A gift, Fabio. Which of my possessions would you choose?'

Fabio did not hesitate. 'Michola,' he said.

Don Paolo's eyes sparked. 'I meant within reason, Fabio.'

'Even so,' said Fabio and he stared the Don out.

Michola, Don Paolo's only child, was a rather husky girl and also prone to sneering. 'Marry your musical peasant?' she said. 'He stinks of fish.'

Nevertheless, the wedding took place.

Within months, Don Paolo accused Fabio of trying to supplant him. 'I am the only Don here,' he said, fingering a silver-hilted stiletto. He tried to skewer Fabio but failed and placed a contract on him instead.

Michola chose that moment to run away with a subservient bandit chief she claimed she had always loved. Thus rejected twice, Fabio fled into the hills.

Contracts sometimes bite back and several that Fabio negotiated on behalf of his father-in-law did just that. The dissatisfied parties were the powerful Giuliano family and they demanded a rearrangement.

Don Paolo sent messages to Fabio, 'My son, you are forgiven,' but Fabio kept his distance and Don Paolo had to renegotiate alone.

Eyewitnesses declare that he was 'stuck like a pig' as he entered the Giuliano boardroom and, after declaring the meeting closed, the directors removed the Don's head and hung his body from their walls before releasing it into the river that flowed beneath.

Fabio descended from the hills, consolidated the holdings that, as the Don's son-in-law, he felt were now his by right. After retrieving Michola from the bandit, he referred to himself as Don Fabio, as if repossession of his predecessor's daughter lent legitimacy. He organised a commemoration for her father, at which he gave the eulogy. He claimed Don Paolo's love for him was uncomplicated and pure, unlike that of fickle women.

Michola said nothing but a smile froze over her face and remained throughout the service. Her thoughts might be surmised from her reaction at the ensuing feast, when Fabio included a selection of his naked leaps and flings, in time to reckless reels from his skirling pipes. 'How glorious was great Don Fabio today,' she said. 'Displaying himself to servant girls like a cocksure rent boy.'

His uilleann pipes were silent but Fabio still swayed to their music. 'I can do far worse,' he slurred. 'So that I might even despise myself. But I'll tell you this,' he waved an uncertain arm at the gathering still around them, 'these servant girls would be glad to have me.'

Michola spat at his feet. 'Then let them share your bed,' she said. 'For I never will again.'

'Not much happened when you did,' said Fabio.

With the collaboration of the local priest, Father Nathaniel, he petitioned for a decree of nullity. On the day it was granted, Fabio despatched Michola to her bandit then visited his old home, where he nodded at his father and sisters then kissed his mother. She clamped him to her bosom as he began to weep.

Tears dried, Fabio climbed to the wind-battered headland of his boyhood dreams, carrying his uilleann pipes. He played the first lament his mother had taught him, dragging his feet from side to side in time with the music, then raised the pipes skywards and hurled them as far as he could. He heard a few strangled drones as they snatched on obstacles then a faint, final smack as they met the sea.

Fabio became a patron of the church. Father Nathaniel had assured him of God's ear, so Fabio used him as a sounding board whenever he felt his business plans might edge into the unethical. As approval appeared automatic, Fabio began to consider God as a sort of spiritual partner.

The Giulianos remained bellicose and the dispute reached crisis point midway through a summer. Mindful of Don Paolo's sudden demise, Fabio sent his capo, Federico, and the cream of his executive to secure his interests against that family's ambitions. He thought his own skills were better kept at home.

One evening, he was resting on his bed after enjoying a young-vatted Verdicchio. He rose and stretched then sniffed noisily, inhaling the combined scents of jasmine and the *rosa moschata* that wound past his window towards the eaves. He almost remembered something, a vision of Michola's pale limbs in fading sunlight perhaps, but it did not linger. He sneezed then sneezed again. 'Fresh air, Don Fabio. You need air.'

He unlocked a door that brought him out onto the roof. A leaded walkway followed the perimeter, guarded by a stone parapet. Fabio strolled along the leads to a position vertically above the jasmine and the rose, opened his flies, stood eloquently on tiptoe and sprinkled the blossoms.

He chose the long walk home. The house was a labyrinth of secrets and the roof snaked this way and that, looking out over lesser roofs, cool strands of water and the occasional *giardino segreto*. He was passing one of the latter, a leafy haven with a small pool, scarcely paying attention, when he heard a splash. He looked down; saw something shimmering, caught in the flat rays of the dying sun. As he watched, a woman reached out to a handrail at the pool's end. Her face was pale, pleasantly proportioned and framed by hair as black as his Arabian mare's. As she pulled herself up from the water, Fabio saw the woman was as naked as his lust, which was expanding with each unblinking second. As if she sensed his intrusion, she began looking about her like a nervous blackbird and when she at last turned her eyes upward, her hands flew to cover her mouth.

Fabio rang for his major domo, took him up to the roof.

The man squinted and said, 'Isn't that the house of Giovanni Motta? His wife is called Alessandra.'

Fabio smiled and the major domo stepped three paces backwards.

'Ah, Giovanni Motta,' said Fabio. 'My pious lieutenant.'

He had her brought to him at midnight. He gasped at the sight of her - at a distance he had thought her beautiful but close to, he saw that impression was wretchedly inadequate. Alessandra's face was such as would stir a man to valiant deeds. She wore a white nightshift, nothing on her feet, and she trembled constantly and kept wringing her hands as though she might be rid of him that way. Fabio enjoyed a sudden fancy that she was a fallen angel and that through her loins he might reach heaven.

'I won't hurt you,' he said, and stepped towards her.

Still shaking, Alessandra backed away until the wall prevented her, then she steadied herself, glared at him. 'Giovanni Motta is my husband. He is away fighting your battles.'

Fabio felt the resentment behind her words and within her deep, dark eyes. All thoughts of angels left his head. 'And I am Don Fabio,' he said. 'I make the rules. I decide who lives, who dies.'

She bit her lip, hung her head and allowed her arms to droop too, so he had to raise each one to pull her shift free. He hurled it to the floor and raised her head by yanking her hair, forcing her to look at him. He saw not reproach now but the fear of a hunted doe. 'I won't hurt you,' he said again, and decided to let her go. Then he looked at her body and knew he could not. 'One night, Alessandra,' he said. 'Just one night.'

Months passed and, though her husband was still absent, Fabio never sought Alessandra again. She wasn't his first reinterpretation of *jus primae noctis*; after Michola rejected him so publicly, he had misused the maidservants he'd boasted about. Several children had been conceived through them even if, in Fabio's mathematics, such offspring didn't count. So he shouldn't have been surprised when Alessandra told him she was pregnant, but nevertheless his face dropped. 'How could you let it happen?'

'As I recall, I didn't have a choice.' Her voice was steady and there was no fear in her eyes now, or reproach. 'I want what is best for my child.'

Fabio sent orders to Federico. Send Giovanni Motta home. A special mission.

When Giovanni arrived, Fabio questioned him about the dispute, how they were coping.

'It's bad…' Giovanni began, and Fabio took notes.

'You've done well, Giovanni Motta,' he said eventually and closed his notebook with a snap. Giovanni blinked. 'The kitchen has orders to spoil you. Eat, drink what you will, then surprise your wife.'

Giovanni gave a short bow then left, but never made the short journey home.

When Fabio heard this next morning, he summoned Giovanni. 'An officer of mine sleeping with servants,' he snorted and an uninterpretable expression crossed Giovanni's face. 'Why did you not go home?'

Giovanni raised his chin. 'While my comrades sleep comfortless in rutted fields, I will not lie in a feather bed. Not for you, Don Fabio, not for anyone.'

Fabio remembered why this man was called 'the pious one'. 'You're a fool, Giovanni Motta,' he said. 'I could have you killed for insolence.' He yawned, lay back, stretching his arms wide. 'However, I admire your courage. All right. Tomorrow you may return to your precious men.' He uncorked a Chianti classico. 'But today you'll drink with me.' Fabio poured wine until he judged Giovanni was anyone's for the taking. 'Now go home and serve your wife.'

Still Giovanni refused.

Next morning, Fabio wrote to Federico. He sealed the envelope and placed it in Giovanni's hand. 'Make sure this reaches him,' he said.

He rang for his major domo. 'Giovanni Motta slept at home last night,' he said.

The major domo nodded, kept his gaze away from Fabio's. 'Naturally,' he said.

News arrived that several of Federico's best men had been ambushed and killed when they took a wrong turning. Giovanni Motta was among them.

Fabio visited the bereaved families. 'It happens,' he said to Alessandra. 'Giovanni was a brave man, just doing his duty. I'm sorry.'

Though her eyes were swollen from crying, Alessandra showed such dignity that Fabio felt she was the Don and he still a simple musician.

'And will you do your duty?' she said.

As Alessandra's body swelled, people began to talk about how it was such a tragedy that her husband had been killed before he saw his only child. Fabio listened, then announced that he would not only assume financial care of the grieving widow but would also marry her and thus give a hero's child a father. The gossip turned to how generous their Don was to foster another man's child, no matter how beautiful the widow.

At the appropriate time, a boy was born to Alessandra and she named him Alessandro. Father Nathaniel called to make the baptismal arrangements and was shown into the business room. When Fabio and Alessandra entered, the priest had his back towards them, and was arranging and rearranging flowers in a tall urn.

Finally he turned and said, 'It is the custom for a firstborn boy to be named after his father.'

Alessandra did not flinch. 'And I choose to break it,' she said.

Father Nathaniel stared at her for a while, then nodded. 'A story,' he said. 'Two men, one rich, one poor. The rich man was successful in everything he did, had many assets, huge tracts of land, while the poor man had nothing except a wife. The rich man had been foolish enough to lose his. One day while the poor man was far from home, the rich man took his wife. Now what do you think of that?'

'It's a lousy story,' said Fabio.

The priest shook his head slowly. 'Oh, Fabio, Fabio,' he said.

'What?' said Fabio but he avoided Father Nathaniel's stare.

'You had all Don Paolo owned,' said the priest. 'Was that too little, Fabio?'

'No.'

'Yet you make Giovanni's wife your own.'

'I wanted to help,' said Fabio after he and Alessandra exchanged glances.

'By killing her husband?'

Fabio laughed yet it echoed in his ears like a cockcrow. 'I have killed many men, Father, yet you and God said nothing. Why accuse me now? Giovanni was one of my own.'

'Precisely,' said the priest.

'Then why should I wish to kill him?'

'Because he refused to sleep with his wife when you brought him home for that purpose.'

Fabio heard Alessandra gasp. He tried to squeeze her hand but she had moved beyond his reach.

'If Giovanni had lived,' said the Father. 'Everyone would know Alessandra was an adulteress.'

Alessandra's lips moved, releasing silent words. The priest seemed not to notice but Fabio understood each one. They were: rape; not adultery but rape.

Her mute protest touched him and he opened his mouth to say the words aloud for her. For that brief moment he was Fabio the peasant, but Don Fabio soon regained control. 'Giovanni was killed by the Giulianos,' he said. 'You know that, Father.'

'Yes, yes. A hundred leagues from here.'

'So what are you saying?'

'That murder is not always direct.'

Fabio's lips thinned and he twisted the new wedding ring on his finger. 'On my son's life,' he said. 'I swear I am innocent of Giovanni Motta's death.' He looked at his wife.

Alessandra said nothing, stared straight ahead beyond the priest, where the only things to see were a shroud-white wall and dead chrysanthemums in a funeral vase.

Watching the Faces

Broughton's hatchet man flicks you a Judas glance and makes the announcement. You stand beside him, irrelevant, watching the faces. You feel the tang of their fear, sense it ebb during the sweeteners then flow again as they realise nothing has really changed and their futures remain uncertain.

The last words are said. The speaker leaves and the faces remain. Their eyes bore into yours. You seek Cathy's, share her pain and flash your sympathy back. Then you return to the others, smile like a waxwork dummy, outwardly unconcerned, though inside you want to hurt someone very badly indeed.

Back in your office, you sink into your chair and, for the first time, feel the full weight of your fifty-two years. You write Giles Broughton on a post-it note, underline the name twice, and shut it in a drawer with the others who have pissed you off over the years.

Cathy comes in. You can see she's trying to be brave. Her face puckers, wanting to cry, and then stiffens as she fights the temptation. 'I guess that's the end for me too,' she says.

'I'm sorry, Cath.' You want to say so much more, reach for her hand.

She takes yours instead. 'It's not your doing, Peter, just Broughton making his mark. It's no big deal. I'm four years from retirement anyway and Frank retires at the end of the year. Couldn't have timed it better really, but what about you?'

'You know I always fancied early retirement.'

'But not yet. And not like this.'

'You know what really hurts?'

Cathy doesn't answer.

'Broughton didn't trust me to tell my own staff. Cath, he didn't fucking trust me.' You shake your head. 'Twenty-five years and I'm not allowed even that dignity.'

Cathy squeezes your hand harder. 'What will Angela say?'

That's worrying you too. 'Probably fly off the handle, blame me.'

Cathy nods, looks thoughtful and you are suddenly reminded of the first time Giles Broughton visited the office. Cathy was impressed with his mix of energy, eloquence and elegance. 'He'll do for me,' she'd said, her face alight.

Looking at her now, you think, Well, Cath, he did that all right.

She's eyeing you curiously. 'Penny for them.'

'Oh, I was just...' But you can't remind her of that, not now. 'It's nothing.'

Cathy gives you a wry smile, shrugs, and goes out. How can she possibly be fifty-six, you wonder.

Broughton's phone rings six times then switches to his secretary's.

'Marie, is Giles there?'

There's silence, then a long sigh. 'I'm sorry, Peter. He's in a meeting. He won't be free all day.'

You sigh too. 'It's all right, Marie, you don't have to pretend.' You put the phone down then groan as someone knocks on your door.

An office junior comes in. 'It's Cathy, sir. She's in the Ladies', sobbing her heart out.' She looks at you as if it's all your fault.

You take Cathy to a restaurant outside town. It's in an Elizabethan mansion, set amongst lush spring meadows. Frightfully expensive but what the hell. You order fresh mullet, their finest Chablis. Cathy's eyes are bright. She looks so elegant in navy blue. She smells of the perfume you bought her last Christmas and you think of the kisses you exchanged then. All very innocent until Angela walked in and misunderstood. Christmas seems a lifetime ago now.

You drink too much wine and later, in the lounge, order coffee. You sit in a quiet corner and...you don't know how it started but this is more serious than Christmas. You're kissing like a couple of teenagers, exploring, devouring each other. But you know it's only the wine – the upset – that perfume.

Somehow you reach the office without being breathalysed.

Now you're faced with Cathy saying, 'What are we going to do?'

'Not much we can do, is there? Get another job, I suppose.'

'I meant about us.'

You look at her dark eyes, mournful now whereas in the restaurant they glittered. You've dreamed of a moment like this but now it's here it doesn't seem so appealing. An image of Angela forms in your head. She is naked, but mocking and unreachable as you grovel, impotent, at her feet. The image fades; you look at Cathy then at the door. You think about making a dash for it.

'We don't need to lose touch,' you say. 'There's the social club, the pensioners' lunches.'

'I didn't mean the pensioners' bloody lunches.'

'I know.'

And it happens. On the beige and mustard carpet tiles. It doesn't take long. Afterwards Cathy looks shocked and so, you expect, do you.

Giles Broughton is still unavailable. You have been shut out, already an outsider.

You think about how easily life tips over. Only two years before, Broughton was the redundant one, made surplus by a takeover. He needed a job, so he was given one, over your head, a job that never existed before. The fact that he and the chairman happened to have been at Winchester together was of course entirely coincidental.

You busy yourself with meetings, counsel staff, arrange relocations. Their prospective managers drown you with platitudes but you know they'll favour their own people. You'd do the same in their position, so why does it grate so much?

Colleagues cross the street to avoid you. You want to shout out, 'It's not contagious,' but you know they're afraid it might be.

Cathy and you avoid each other too. Difficult when she is only feet away. You hear her closing filing cabinets, tapping her keyboard, talking over the phone. She no longer brings you coffee.

You try not to think about what happened.

It is a week before you tell Angela.

'They've sacked you?' Her face is white, her knuckles tight.

'Not sacked,' you say, far too quickly. 'Early retirement.' You tell her about lump sums, commutations.

Her eyes glaze over. 'Peter,' she says. 'Why, for Christ's sake?'

You wait for the tirade to start but suddenly her lips quiver. She looks vulnerable then and you remember why you fell in love with her. You want to confess about Cathy, tell her it didn't mean anything.

'Downsizing,' you say. 'Lose billions developing shopping centres nobody wants, cut your losses by shedding staff. In this case, the perceived remedy is to close the out-of-town head office. Ergo, one surplus executive director.'

'And his secretary.'

You wince inside, don't need reminding. 'And his secretary.'

Angela says, 'Cathy's too damned attractive for my liking.'

Cathy gets a job with her husband's firm. 'Just till Frank retires.'

You have to ask. 'Does he know?'

She looks you straight in the eyes. 'Nothing happened, Peter.'

When she leaves, you walk her down to the street. Frank is waiting.

You and Cathy hug each other. 'I'll miss you.'

Cathy's crying as she gets into the car. Frank stares at you for a while, man to man, then nods and drives away.

You catch the next London train.

'Peter!' Broughton's secretary looks alarmed.

'It's all right, Marie, I won't kill him. Not yet.'

She grins then. 'He's on his own.' She nods towards the inner door.

'Giles,' you say, unable to keep the flutter from your voice. 'It's time you stopped ignoring me.'

Broughton is remarkably calm. You suppose it's the Winchester education. 'Ah, Peter, there you are,' he says, as if he'd mislaid you for a moment. 'Nice to see you. Sit down, please.' He rings for tea.

Marie puts the tray down, winks at you as she leaves. Broughton pours two cups, milk second. You tell him you can't face an empty desk for six months. That you want out right now. Garden leave.

'Perfectly understandable, Peter. I've been there myself, remember.' He is so nice. His enunciation, manners, clothes, aftershave are exquisite. He listens patiently, agrees to everything, and shakes your hand firmly as you leave.

In the lift, you realise that you've just done exactly what Broughton wanted. After going through the swivel doors, you spin them hard, watch until they stop. Then you spin them again.

You can keep the Jaguar. Angela is relieved. She doesn't want the neighbours to know you're redundant. She gives a little shiver as she says 'redundant'.

'Why should that matter? Christ, Angela, we'll hardly be on the breadline. For the first time in our lives, we can do whatever we want. We could buy a cottage, move to the country.'

Angela flares up. 'If you think I'm living in pig shit…' And things go from bad to worse. She has her coffee mornings, she says, her afternoon golf. 'People come here. I don't want you cluttering up the house.'

You sign up with an agency, fill in forms. Twenty-year-old consultants ask about your 'skill set'.

Each morning Angela kisses you a public goodbye before you drive the company's car to nowhere. Each night she says, 'I'm too tired' and you're downsized again.

You spend hours travelling – smart shirt, best suit, polished shoes – try to impress people half your age. The agency always says, 'Yes, the client likes you,' but somehow this never translates into a job. You tell them to remove you from their list.

The Jaguar crouches in the garage, never springing out. Angela cancels her coffee mornings and makes her golf last all day. You slump in a chair, watch *Oprah* and *Neighbours*.

Each night your dream is the same: you drive to work but Security won't lift the barriers and let you in. You blast your horn, insist that you're the boss and finally they relent but when you get inside the building and reach your floor, you see your office being pulled down. You are cold, shivering and the faces are staring at you, pointing. You realise that you are wearing only a pyjama jacket, no trousers. Office girls snigger and you wake suddenly. Your hair, pillows, sheets, nightclothes are soaked with sweat. Far away across the bed, Angela moans in her sleep.

Soon you only shave twice a week. You live in frayed shirts, ancient Levis, dilapidated Nikes. Angela tells the neighbours you are on sick leave then tries to make you see a doctor.

You begin to take a drink, lunchtimes at first, then stretching into the afternoon, and finally the whole of one black day when you brood on a barstool about the symbols that once proclaimed who you were – the best Jag; the office with the view of the girls sunbathing topless below; first-class everything wherever you went. You think how, when people meet for the first time, they always ask each other, 'What do you do?' as if a job is all that defines anyone. Well, what exactly defines you now?

'Fuck all,' you say and start to laugh.

The barman looks at you as if you're one of the winos on the bench outside.

'Downsized, squire,' you tell him. 'I'm – terminally – bloody – downsized.'

You almost make it home. Your next-door neighbour finds you sprawled on the pavement at the corner of your road. You try to explain that you're downsized and he says you mustn't worry. He lets you use his shoulder as a crutch.

Angela bawls at you. 'You're a useless, drunken sod. I hate you. Christ, it'll be all over the close by now.'

She throws a Doulton shepherdess her mother bought then weeps as it lies in pieces on the floor. Then she beats her fists angrily against your chest. Her face looks wild and you suddenly grab hold of her wrists, force them to be still. As you pull her towards you, a strange excitement arrives in her eyes. You feel so hard it's frightening and you make love for the first time in months.

Afterwards you promise. No drinking. Yes, I'll phone another agency. You kiss Angela's soft, chestnut hair and tell her that you love her. She is soft and warm and inviting. You wonder why you ever thought she was any different.

You fill in new forms, another CV.

Someone called Sophie phones you at home. 'We've arranged an interview. I'm sorry that it's such short notice.'

You don't even have time to iron a shirt.

A young woman greets you. She is fair-haired, neat, nice smile. She says she is Sarah from HR. She is good. She makes it seem like conversation but all the time she is making notes, quizzing you. She finally leaves you alone with a plastic cup of coffee and comes back with a tall man. He is young, about twenty-eight.

'I'm Werner,' he says. There is just the trace of an accent.

He has few questions, mostly stares at your CV. You probe, but Werner is vague. It is a new company, to do with acquisitions, he says. He doesn't explain further and soon you are tired of asking. As you stand up to leave, there is a knock on the door.

A girl comes in. 'Have you lost something, Werner?' She has a man's jacket over her arm.

Werner checks the label on the one he is wearing. He looks bemused. 'This isn't mine,' he says.

'Thought not,' says the girl. She hands him the jacket.

Werner searches the pockets, takes out a cellphone. 'I wondered where that was,' he says.

You wonder why you came at all.

Angela has dinner ready, poached beef in St Emilion. She hands you a glass of the wine.

'I have a good feeling about this job,' she says.

You wish you had such confidence but with the help of the wine you soon approach euphoria; Angela is radiant and you fall in love with her all over again.

'If things turn out well, maybe we could buy that cottage,' she says. 'Just for weekends, you understand.'

As you uncork a second bottle, the phone rings.

'It's Sophie from the agency,' Angela says and shows you that she has her fingers crossed.

You expect the familiar run-around, but this time it is different. You put the phone down, grab Angela and dance her around the room. 'They've offered me the bloody job,' you say.

Much later you remember that you don't know what it is.

When you do find out, you realise that you still have principles. Loyalty weighs itself against the desire for revenge. The company is the UK subsidiary of a huge Swiss concern. Werner is the son of its president. He was truthful when he mentioned acquisitions. Number one on his list is your ex-employer and you realise it isn't you they want, but your insider's knowledge.

Angela says, 'Where's your problem, Peter? They shit on you, remember.'

You mumble something about professional ethics.

She says, 'Bollocks. You didn't think about that when you were getting pissed out of your skull.'

Or when I was screwing my secretary, you think as you avoid Angela's stare. Then you think of the people still employed there. Some you've known for twenty-five years. You find yourself caring about their hopes, their families. Werner assured you their jobs would be safe. 'Provided they add value,' he said.

In your head, it begins to make sense. Your old firm is a minor player in a sector it once dominated. The investment from Werner's company would shunt it back towards the top. Without that stimulus, the jobs might be lost anyway.

The best half of a bottle of Glenfiddich later, you allow yourself to dream. You enjoy the expression on Broughton's face as you tell him to clear his desk. Werner hinted you might do that. Ecce loyalty and revenge, mutually compatible. You smile at the thought then remember the interview with Werner. How the hell can you trust a man who doesn't know whose clothes he is wearing?

Angela has disappeared upstairs and you think about what she said about moving to the country. Only for weekends, but that could change. Somewhere with land – you could keep chickens, grow trees. There's just the little problem of persuading her about not taking the job.

She comes into the room. 'It's late,' she says. She's wearing the nightdress, the smile you remember from years ago.

You put the cork back into the bottle.

'Have you decided?'

'Mmm.'

'You'll accept the job?'

'I'll phone Werner in the morning.' You hope your eyes didn't flicker.

Priest in Kilvarnet

> When I play on my fiddle in Dooney,
> Folk dance like a wave of the sea;
> My cousin is priest in Kilvarnet,
> My brother in Moharabuiee.
>
> W.B. Yeats

My cousin is Priest in Kilvarnet. Or rather that's what he says he is. I know he's never been nearer Kilvarnet than the high road out of Cloncarmel. And as for the priesthood, the closest he's been to a church these last twenty years is sweeping the pavements outside St Kilda's in Dundonnell Road. And that was only for the three days he managed to turn up for work, the last time he came out of Mountjoy gaol.

What my cousin Seamais actually is, is a conman, a blagger, a piss artist who wouldn't know how to speak the truth if it flew out of his mouth wearing angel's wings. But how he became this bogus, this surrogate priest, the physical progress so to speak, was like this.

It was always his mammy's wish to have a priest in the family, and now with her close to dying from an over-affinity with Paddy's eyewater, my cousin Seamais has discovered an inclination to indulge her. And so he mugged poor old Father Kilkenny as he came off the Holyhead boat at Dunlaoghaire one night and took his dog collar and holy stuff and the Bushmills single malt the poor man had been trying to fight off the seasickness with. As a result of the latter infliction, the good father might not have been as keen-eyed as he is when clocking who's at Mass and who isn't.

Then Seamais, bold as you like, went round to St Catherine's Hospital where me old Aunty Annie, his blessed mother, was lying. He said he'd come to give her the last rites. He poured her a shot of Bushmills and she smiled at him as if all the bells of glory were pealing out in her head. She told Seamais if there was a happier woman in all the world, she'd fight her to prove she wasn't.

But there must have been something about Seamais that made the ward sister suspicious. Maybe it was the stink of stale Guinness for he still had his old clothes on under Father Kilkenny's stuff. Anyway she came chuffing out of the nurses' station like the Belfast express and said plain, 'Who the shite are you?' or words to the same effect. A bit cleaner maybe.

'Why, I'm the priest in Kilvarnet,' said Seamais, as cool as Liffey water.

'Funny,' said the sister, 'Kilvarnet's a Church of Ireland parish and your woman there is as Catholic as the Pope himself, God bless him.'

'Ah now, that might have been true up to last week,' began Seamais but then his old mother gave a croak and started to bubble at the mouth. 'Would you have some concern for a dying woman,' Seamais hissed at the sister, who came over all starched proficiency then and waved her arms at the other nurses.

'Quickly,' she said, 'get the screens round her.'

But old Annie sat up straighter than a justice of the peace. 'I'm not bloody dyin' yet,' she said. 'It's that holy water me son the priest gave me. It went down the wrong way, that's all.'

The sister looked as if she wanted to go home. She looked at Seamais and then she looked at his mother. 'Ah yes, Mrs O'Leary,' she said. 'But it seems to have worked a miracle while it was about it.'

'There you are, son,' said old Annie to Seamais. 'A priest today – you'll be a fuckin' saint next week.'

Well, the poor sister couldn't help herself, Seamais tells me. Her mouth twisted fit to bust and she nearly choked with the laughing. Then she scuttled off with her shoulders still heaving and from the way she was walking he says it looked as if she'd peed herself too.

But the big thing, Seamais swears, is that Annie's given up on the dying – a miracle indeed. Why, she could well be home within the week.

I can see he believes it, like he believes all the blarney he utters. This time, though, he's only conning himself.

And that's how, if only in his Mammy's eyes, my cousin is Priest in Kilvarnet.

Is summer coming early?

The morning after his wife flew Stateside to visit her mother, my neighbour Jack Ritchey unloaded a lawnmower from Wanda Cipollini's car. Wanda high-heeled behind him into the house and within ten minutes its windows were curtained tight. Over the next three days, nothing changed. Then on the fourth – it must have been early because I was sniffing out what sort of day it was – Jack put the mower in Wanda's trunk. As she drove away, I wondered why he'd taken it out in the first place. Mowers are heavy things to lift, more so when you don't need to.

Jack called round later. 'Hi, Hawk,' he said.

I didn't mention Wanda though Jack looked as if he thought I might. His windows were wide open, curtains drawn back and twitching in a breeze that brewed stronger as the day warmed.

'Letting fresh air in,' said Jack, scratching an ear. 'Nadine flies into Heathrow today. We're stopping over at the Hilton there.' He play-punched me in the stomach. 'Hey, old buddy. Keep an eye on things while I'm away? You never know these days.' He grinned but it looked like he was blushing too.

I was running my old push mower over my grass when Jack arrived with Nadine. I'd got as far as thinking of cutting theirs.

Nadine waved as if she'd been away years, and sixteen stones of irrepressible woman gushed across the driveway we'd shared since she backed their VW through our dividing fence. She slopped kisses on my cheek and crushed me into the cushions of her chest.

'Jeez, Nadine!' Jack said. 'You'll smother the poor guy.'

'So then he'll die happy.'

As Jack straightened a cherry-red baseball cap over his semi-crew,

Nadine noticed the lawn. 'Jack Ritchey, I said get this cut before I come home.'

Jack muttered something about the Yard Boy breaking down.

'You could've borrowed Hawkshaw's here,' Nadine said. 'Or is that too much like hard work?' She peered at me then, closer than I liked, as if she hadn't looked properly before. 'You eaten while I've been away, Hawk? You've gotten far too thin.'

'It was only a few days,' I said.

'Five,' Nadine said and invited me for supper.

I wasn't the only guest. I watched Jack wilt as Wanda walked in with a tower block.

'Leroy, my man,' Jack said to the block.

They slapped palms.

Leroy was at least six-six with muscles everywhere and I wondered why Wanda would even think of humping skimpy Jack. She was sexy in that obvious way lazy guys like him go for: smooth olive-skin, dark wayward tresses, pensive eyes. 'Trailer trash,' Nadine called her, swore 'that natural tan's nuttin' but natural dirt'. Wanda had chosen a modest sleeveless dress and combed her hair into submission, fixed it with a big tortoiseshell grip but she couldn't prevent those contours shifting under the thin cotton. Jeez, I felt myself wanting her too.

Jack caught me Wanda-watching as Nadine served tacos and enchiladas. My cheeks were near boiling as he waggled an 'O' with a thumb and finger.

Nadine missed that but saw me all right. 'Chilli too hot, Hawk?' she said and poured me some iced water.

We played Aggravation at a table that was pockmarked from dice. Not a smooth surface anywhere. Leroy wore a smile that worried me as he tussled with Jack and won what turned out to be the final game.

'That's your ass whupped, motherfucker.' Wanda bounced up and down so fast my eyes dislocated.

'What did you call my husband?'

Wanda flung Nadine's glare back. 'It was a figure of speech.'

'Yeah? Well, it was the wrong figure, lady.'

Sweat beaded across Jack's forehead and Wanda, eyelashes slung low, muttered something I couldn't catch.

'Hey, Princess.' Leroy's voice was as deep and dark as Suffolk clay. 'We're on a visit. That's no way to talk to a lady.'

'As if you'd know.' Wanda's lips quivered and she rained tiny fists over Leroy's iron pectorals.

They left after that and Nadine went into the kitchen. To load the dishwasher, she said.

Jack poured a Jim Beam. He was still sweating. 'Want one, old buddy?' he said, waving the bottle towards me.

'I'll stick to Coke.' I went to fetch one from the cool box.

Nadine hadn't touched the dishes but was sorting through laundry I guessed Jack was supposed to do while she was away. She looked as if she'd be some time. I gave up on the Coke and said 'Goodnight' instead.

'Goodnight, Hawk,' Nadine said. She didn't look up.

At work next day, I got a message from Jack asking if I'd join him for a drink in the Airmen's Club. I teach school on the American base where he's stationed. I used to think my Cambridge MA guaranteed the kids the culture they wouldn't get at home. But that was before my life messed up.

Jack was there first. 'One won't hurt,' he said, sliding a whiskey towards me.

'Maybe not,' I said. 'Now, what's the story, Jack?'

'Is there one?'

'Jack, this is Hawk you're talking to. You're not in Possum Holler now.'

His sigh spanned a lifetime. 'I really was borrowing the Yard Boy but I offered Wanda a beer. She came in, stared at me in that way she has. Jeez, they were leaping at me.'

'But three days, Jack?'

Jack took his time working up a grin. 'One ain't enough with Wanda.'

'What the hell did she see in you?'

'You ain't God's friggin' gift. I saw you check her out. Don't tell me you'd say no.'

84

'But I'm not married any more, Jack.'

Jack's grin disintegrated. 'I thought, what the hell, Nadine'll never know.'

'What if Leroy does?'

'He don't,' said Jack. 'He'd of killed me by now for sure.'

I thought about Wanda's car stuck in Jack's drive for anyone to see. Jack's right eyelid began twitching. I passed him my untouched whiskey and turned my back on him, watched some women dancing.

Jack tapped my shoulder. 'Blonde or brunette?'

'Brunette.'

A foxy smile cracked his face. 'The blonde is Captain Stablinski. Let's split them up.'

The dark-haired girl was English like me, but had breeding. 'I'm Catherine Levaux,' she said, 'and yes, I'll dance with you.' She cocked her head at her companion.

'Do what you like.' The words came ready-clipped, with a sour delivery.

Jack smiled in a way I wasn't sure I liked. He stooped and said, 'Would you dance with me, Captain?'

'Taking the piss, Ritchey?'

He jerked to a slack-shouldered attention. 'No, ma'am. I was asking if you'd like to dance. Seeing as your friend will be dancing with my friend Hawkshaw here.'

Captain Stablinski snapped a glance at me and raised her eyebrows. 'Step on my feet, Sergeant, and you're dead.'

The music was country sputter but my dad would have loved it. I was doing fine until my dick stiffened against Catherine's tight, too close belly. I mumbled sorries but she laughed, 'So that's how things stand.' We began talking like people who knew each other then and I asked if I could see her again. Captain Stablinski zoomed our way and Catherine seemed to freeze.

'Levaux Opticians,' she said under her breath. 'It's in the book.'

'I meant socially.'

'I know.'

Captain Stablinski looked me up and down. 'My friend Janey,' she said, 'married a local national with a damn-fool name like yours.' Her three-quarter sneer told me where I'd seen her before and that had me strung up tighter than the divorce lawyer's knots ever managed.

I made for the door, coattails swishing in my wake. I heard glass break and Jack's voice, 'Let him go, I'll take care of that.'

'Was it something I didn't say?' Catherine had caught up with me.

'No.'

We followed a line of trees towards the base housing, talked about nothing that mattered until I said, 'How did you meet Captain Stablinski?' Catherine's cheeks flamed but before she could respond a woman shot across our path so fast she almost achieved lift-off.

'Get your ass back here, Cipollini.'

Wanda cornered like a street racer, accelerated into a maze of parking lots I knew lay behind the houses.

'Leroy?'

He stared as if I wasn't in his database then his brow twitched and he thumped his great fists together with a force that made me wince. 'Hawkshaw,' he bawled. He lifted me clean off the ground and I knew I was about to shit myself to death. In a whisper that would raise goosebumps on a saint, he said, 'Hawkshaw, I got no quarrel with you,' and dropped me. He shuffled away and I wiped spittle from my face.

Catherine looked as if she'd seen Beelzebub himself. 'Oh God, Hawkshaw,' she said. 'I wet myself.'

Jack grumbled like drunks do and by the time I separated him from the bar Catherine had vanished. I took Jack to an inn that wasn't particular then called Nadine on his mobile. 'Leroy's been here,' she said, 'mad as a moose with toothache, said he's gonna whip Jack's dick right off of him, feed it to his dog. I told him, you don't got a dog and he said he'd make sure and get one. Just for this.'

'Did he say why?'

'You're gonna tell me.'

'Sorry, Nadine, signal's breaking up.'

Nadine screwed one eye up, pinioned me with the other. 'Took you long enough.'

'Didn't know I was being timed.'

She looked drawn, thin for a fat lady. 'What went on between Jack and Wanda?'

It was hard to make out my feet in the dark.

'Don't you boys just clam up! Okay. Tomorrow, if it ain't that already. Just tell me Jack's okay, though why I should care…'

'He's okay. All he did was borrow her mower.'

Nadine gave me a long, hard stare before shutting her door.

As I dropped into sleep, electronic Bach serenaded me. It took me a while to realise it came from Jack's mobile.

'Where's Jack?' I sensed the silent 'fuck it'.

'Making sure Leroy doesn't find him.'

'So you have his phone but he's not with it, right?'

'Right.'

There was a snatch of line noise, or it could have been sniffling.

'Wanda, you okay?'

'No, I'm not. I've been circling Crazyville for hours.'

'You could stay here,' I said, and wished I hadn't. 'For tonight.'

'You mean that? Hawk, I promise you won't regret it.'

As she stepped into my hall, Wanda's head pressed into my shoulder. She cried and swore then gazed up at me. I'd never had her attention before and could see what Jack meant about the way she looked at you. I thought about Leroy feeding my dick to his dog along with Jack's.

'I'll use the sofa,' I said.

Nadine had her hair in fancy coils and wore just enough make-up. She deserved to be told she looked good. 'Always the gentleman,' she said and I thought about what I wanted to do with Catherine and Wanda. Christ, Nadine too, if it came to that.

'What are you thinking of, Hawkshaw Hawkins?'

'I'm thinking I should change my name.'

Nadine twisted her hands together, spent time inspecting them. 'Maybe I should change mine.'

I thought about that as we drove to fetch Jack. I wondered what Janey called herself now.

'What I want is the truth, Jack,' Nadine said. 'You gonna give me that?'

Jack's Adam's apple wobbled and I knew he was about to swing his arms in give-away parallel.

'Nadine,' I said, 'there's something I haven't told you. Jack just covered our tracks. Wanda's and mine. She's at my place right now.

Nadine stared at me then shook her head. 'Well, ain't that the darndest thing?'

Leroy's wrinkled TransAm blocked our drive. I hoped Wanda had the sense to stay indoors.

'Leroy Parker! Out now.' Nadine was like I imagined Boadicea, even had the gold helmet with her hair the way it was.

Leroy death-stared at Jack.

'Look at me, you great sonofabitch.' Nadine torpedoed Leroy's crotch.

'Whaddya do that for?' He took a while unfolding. When he did, one hand shielded his balls while the other held a bowie knife.

Nadine moved fast for a big woman. As Leroy released a great banshee wail and cannoned towards Jack, she intervened. Leroy slammed into the VW and his knife scored a serpentine motif in its powder-blue paint.

'FREEZE!'

In red corduroy shirt, tight Levis, hair in a yellow band, Wanda made a magnificent brigand. The shotgun was mine; kept under the bed in case Janey came back. I never got round to buying cartridges.

'Sonofafuckingwhore,' Leroy screamed at Jack.

'You've got it wrong, Leroy.' I put an arm around Wanda's waist, hoped she'd understand.

Leroy's brow furrowed. 'You?' He gaped at Wanda then glared at me. He had red-eye, like a bad photograph. 'I shoulda finished you last night. Shoulda porked your Limey dyke too.'

Nadine looked as if she'd throw up. 'Trailer trash,' she said to Wanda, 'Jack and I are leaving. You want to stop us, pull that trigger now.'

Wanda flinched at 'trailer trash' but her eyes didn't flicker as she shook me away and levelled the shotgun at Leroy. 'Tell me again what I am to you.'

'Princess, I didn't mean nothing.'

The gun moved closer.

'Jesus, Princess!'

'Say it!' Wanda's trigger finger tensed.

Leroy mumbled something.

'Louder!'

'A piece of meat with a fuckhole!'

Wanda cracked the shotgun against Leroy's skull. He rocked like a wayward metronome.

'I'm no man's meat,' she said. 'I'm Wanda Cipollini and I make the choices.'

Wanda found some Famous Grouse I hadn't opened in weeks. She raised eyebrows at the empties keeping it company.

'I can take it or leave it.'

'Trouble is when you can't leave it. Right?'

'Right.'

'Maybe I shouldn't encourage you then.' She poured herself a glass and put the bottle away. 'You got plans for today, Hawk?' Her smile said all you have to do is ask.

'Someone to see in town.'

'Scared of being alone with a naked woman?'

My pulse passed two hundred.

'I'm taking a bath,' she said. 'Wash some dirt away.'

Levaux Opticians leaned at an unlikely angle over a mediaeval corner of town. Catherine wore an almost-black skirt and top, matching her eyes and hair and the stained oak beams. 'Oh, it's you,' she said, never slipping into a smile once.

On our way to lunch, she window-shopped, chattered about stuff she'd like to buy. I'd forgotten women did that. But in the pub I chose, Catherine became a frozen Madonna and I sat tongue-tied on grapefruit juice while conversations bubbled around us.

'I'm not good at this,' I said.

'It's me,' she said. 'Not you.' She fiddled with her shoe and her satin top hung open like the gap in my life.

I ached to touch the little breasts I could see nestling in their strapless bra and I wanted to scream at her because she knew that.

Captain Stablinski was waiting when I walked Catherine back. I stayed outside, looked through the window. My reflection glared back, segmented by slatted blinds. I looked as if I'd seen enough.

Back home was a note: At the commissary. Love Wanda. I knew 'love' meant nothing but it comforted me. I checked out life next door.

Jack managed a quick 'Thanks, old buddy' before Nadine started down the stairs. Her Boadicea curls were now threshed hay.

'I came to say sorry,' I said. 'You know I mess up with women.'

Nadine sighed like a slow puncture. 'You pick the wrong ones.' Outside an engine died, popping its exhaust. 'There's another now. Needs a tailpipe.' She began to laugh. 'You get that, Hawk? Wanda needs a new tailpipe.'

Wanda clasped the bottle, swallowed whiskey by the neck. She looked hag-ridden. 'Leroy came out the PX, waving that knife, made one crazy dash at me, yelling all he said before and worse. Women squealed like hogs. Then there were guns everywhere.'

'Where is he now?'

'Sweeping shit in Georgia. I told Nancy Stablinski most of what's happened.'

'Captain Stablinski?'

'My boss.'

'She danced with Jack.'

'With Jack? Now that I'd pay to see.'

That lightened her up and she cooked *orecchiette con quattro formaggi*. 'My grandmamma's special recipe. From Cortona.' Whatever the truth, the result smelled like heaven and tasted better.

'I'm through with the military this summer,' Wanda said, midway through the second bottle of Valpolicella she reckoned I could risk. 'Leroy went ape-shit when he found out and Jack's seemed the best place to hide. Especially with Nadine away.' Wanda lowered her eyes. 'Ninety-nine per cent of the time we were drinking though I'd bet Jack said different.' She stared into nowhere, nibbling her bottom lip and tapping her fingers, one against one. 'You know, a trailer would have been luxury to me. My daddy worked hard but jobs were scarce. In between them he drank, stuck Momma with a kid each year. Used to try on me too.' She settled her eyes on mine. 'Nadine's right. I am trash.'

'No, Wanda, life just dealt lousy cards.'

'Even so. Never wished you could lose your past?'

'They say accepting it makes you strong.' I forgot to add I didn't believe that shit but I did tell her about my wife.

'I never connected Janey Hawkins with you,' Wanda said. 'Another man's one thing, but…' She untied her hair and I saw it knew exactly where to fall.

I grinned at the new morning, listened to Wanda's soft moans as she shifted in her sleep, marvelled to feel her warm body instead of cold sheet. A ribbon of spring stole through a gap in the curtains and lit Wanda's face. I stroked her hair, ran it through my fingers, memorised each filament.

The telephone rang and Wanda woke with a start, blinking as her eyes met sunlight. She seemed surprised to see me and reached for the duvet then let it drop, peered from the sides of her eyes. Her nipples swelled from their mysterious dark circles like fat buds on an exotic flower. Her cheeks flushed.

The telephone rang again and kept on. Wanda pursed her lips. 'They ever gonna give us peace? Tell them we got unfinished business.'

The sun hadn't made it this far. The voice was icy too.

'Why didn't you stay?'

'You were busy.'

'I'm calling now, aren't I?'

I kicked, barefoot, at the wall. It hurt enough.

'Hawkshaw, I'm not what you think.'

I heard Wanda on the stairs. 'Honey, y'all okay down there?'

'Catherine, I have to go.' The phone was already dead.

Wanda had showered and dressed. 'I got cold,' she said, 'and Hawk, you got frostbite. That had to be a woman.'

'I could stay with you till summer,' she said later. 'Till they send me home. If you want.'

'I want.'

'What about Catherine?'

'What about her?'

'She bothers you, Hawk.' Wanda threw a Giaconda smile. 'If you need to, just tell me summer's come early. You and me, it's...'

'Just for fun?'

'You said it.' She gazed at the heath beyond my window. 'Hawk, if we'd met five years ago...'

'You weren't here.'

'What the hell, you wouldn't've looked at me twice. I was a gawky kid needing a meal.' She turned and I saw she was blushing. 'Would you call me trailer trash? When we fuck...make love, I mean.'

'Why?'

Wanda shrugged. 'Therapy?'

I sat in Catherine's flat, at a table covered with crisp lace.

'I'm sorry I jumped to conclusions,' she said. 'Nancy said it was kind of you to take Wanda in.' She ran a finger along the tablecloth edge.

'Three cheers for Captain Nancy.'

'Don't be bitter with me.' It was the first time I'd seen her pout. 'Hawkshaw, I thought we were friends.'

'What I don't know, Catherine, is what kind we are, what kind you and Nancy are.'

She was all tight lips, folded arms then suddenly grinned like a cheeky kid. 'Where did you get that damn-fool name?'

'My dad was a bastard.'

'I'm sorry?'

'An American serviceman's. Not Nancy's lot. Navy. Midshipman on a friendship visit.'

Catherine frowned. 'I didn't mean to open…'

'Apart from his conception, the closest Dad got to America was naming me after his favourite country singer. I remember Mum's smirk as she told Dad his hero had died in a plane crash. I was five. Maybe that's why I use Hawkshaw. To her, I was Michael. Maybe that's why I married an American.'

'Is that why you're fucking one?'

'No.'

She stared into a tall gilt-framed mirror.

'Are you and Nancy lovers?'

As our reflected eyes met, she said, 'I don't want her in that way.'

'Catherine,' I said. 'Why do you never give proper answers?'

She began tapping feet. 'You ask the wrong questions.'

'Let's try again. What kind of friends are we, Catherine? You and I?'

I expected a protracted silence but she tutted and stood up.

'I'll show you what kind.'

She discarded clothes as if they were sacks. I had an unhappy sense of déjà vu. A voluptuous curve ran from her slender waist to surprisingly robust hips. She poised like an alabaster Venus then lay down, legs awkwardly apart, dared me to look away.

'Catherine, this isn't right. Not like this.'

'It's what I want. It's why I brought you here.' She sat up. 'I want you to trust me.'

I'd seen her expression on plaster saints above my childhood bed and knew I was about to do anything she asked. Then a much later image interceded: my wife in a car with Nancy Stablinski, who grinned as if she was the keeper of a secret I wouldn't like.

'Catherine,' I said. 'I can't even trust myself.'

I walked home, three miles uphill. It helped me make plans: there were ways round obstacles. I reckoned I could find them all now.

Wanda pulled a face when I walked in. 'Is summer coming early? Will you miss me when it does?'

'About as much as you'll miss me.'

'One hell of a lot then.'

'More than that.'

We hugged each other for a while; dampened our faces and hair.

'Summer's way off yet,' I said.

Then there was the music

Your name is Irena, the only possession you have left. If you lose that, then you truly will be nobody. That is why, when the tractor people found you wandering, you kept it inside your head. Told them nothing, just accepted water, food, and a ride.

Below is a city of white tents, like ghosts in the morning mist.

Rain falls before you reach the valley floor. Ahead is a checkpoint, men in green uniforms. Panic arcs across your breast and you hunch up but the soldiers keep to their shelter, scarcely look as they wave the tractor on towards the border.

You pass through a gateway into the canvas city you saw from the mountain. People mill in muddy aisles. Rain on tent cloth and thousands of voices merge into one amorphous, deafening discordance. You wonder if you will ever get used to it. Soon, you pick out individual voices, realise they speak your language. You breathe a little easier.

People approach: official expressions, jeans, white T-shirts with a logo. They speak with foreign accents, lead you and the tractor people to a desk where a young blonde woman sits and smiles. Her name tag says Jacqueline. Throughout the smiling, her eyes remain cold. When she asks, the tractor people give their names but you just shake your head.

Another tent: latrines and water. You pee then remove your ragged clothes. You long for a shower, a bath, but here are only basins. You scrub yourself with hard yellow soap until your skin glows then scrub harder still. Some dirt stays out of reach. You cry a little then.

You are given black bread, watery soup, clean clothes, a blanket. The T-shirt people escort you to a tent, point to a corner. An old woman smiles, revealing rotten teeth. You wonder where the tractor people are.

Your corner seems safe. You sit on your bed and dream, eyes open, see Mama, hear her singing as she rocks you gently to and fro. You wish Miran was here.

Then far away, you hear someone screaming.

The old woman with the bad teeth strokes your brow. 'There, there, little one. Tikja will take care of you.'

You realise that the screams were your own, but you cannot recall the dreams.

The woman Jacqueline arrives. A young man is with her. She says his name is Jamie. You ignore them, sit on your bed, rocking, try to recall Miran's face.

Days, nights pass.

The young man comes alone. His voice is dark brown and, if you were in the mood, his pronunciation of your language would make you smile. He tells you he used to visit your country, claims to love your mountains, your green valleys. 'I want to help,' he says.

You do not look at his eyes. You wish he would go away. You wish Miran would come.

You had to help Tikja in the morning bread queue and now, late afternoon, she clutches at her chest and slumps on her bed. The man Jamie rushes over, shakes her gently, says her name. He lowers his mouth to hers and breathes life into her lungs.

Tikja was kind to me, you think. She must not die. You race for the tent door while the other women stare like idiots.

Outside, boys are playing football.

'Please, a doctor!' you cry.

They point towards a tent. You run, heart pounding, like you might once have run from the soldiers.

You sit in the hospital tent, think Tikja's eyes look like a crow's, two shining black beads.

She cackles. 'So,' she says, 'My good friend, you saved my life.'

She insists on kissing you. Her breath makes you recoil. You think of that poor man Jamie giving her the kiss of life.

He is there too. He smiles at you and asks your name. You smile back and forget not to look at his eyes. They are blue-green. They look kind.

'Irena Bardici,' you say, then clap a hand to your mouth.

But no wishing can retrieve the words now.

Later, you greet Jamie in his own tongue.

He blinks, shakes his head. 'Sorry?'

'I ask how are you.'

His eyes open wide. 'You speak English?'

'Not so much.'

You tell him about university. How you wanted to travel, teach but you were needed at home.

'Where was that?'

In his own language his voice is treacle and before you know it, you have answered him.

'What happened, Irena?' he whispers. 'What did they do?'

You shiver, tear at your hair. 'No!' you scream. 'No! I can never say.' And you beat your fists against this man who made you remember.

You walk, think of the day you begged Miran not to leave.

'It is my duty,' he said, holding you at arm's length. 'The soldiers will not harm you. We've lived with their people all our lives, cut the hair of each other's firstborn. Teodor will protect you.'

He kissed you then and you cried. Salt tears mixed with his taste. He left without looking back.

Now you cry again. Softly, silently. If you knew, Miran. What would you say to that?

Jamie is waiting when you return. You turn your back on him.

'I'm sorry,' he says.

You try to scream but the sound will not come.

Jamie clears his throat. His eyes are furtive. 'I know about the barn.'

You feel the blood leave your face. 'How can you? You were not there.'

'There are people from your village here.'

'I haven't met them.'

'Irena, there are one hundred thousand refugees here. Seven thousand in this camp alone.'

You clench your fists. 'Don't patronise me. I know that.'

For one long black moment, you hear the machine guns' chatter, the silence afterwards, then flames and smoke, the terrible screaming, silence again. And with the smoke, the stench of burning flesh.

Your heart feels as if it will leap from your chest. You force yourself not to weep.

'I'm sorry,' Jamie says quietly.

He is good at saying sorry, you think. But his eyes seem honest now. You fancy you see compassion there.

'Would you like me to look for your relatives?'

You shrug. 'There is only my husband. It is two months since I saw him.' You look down at your belly, remember you have not yet bled.

'Miran is not here.'

'But he's alive,' you say. 'I would know if he were not.'

Jamie says, 'Sorry,' again. It must be his favourite word.

'Don't be sorry for me. Many of our people suffer more.'

'Perhaps you could help them?'

'What do you mean?'

'Act as interpreter when we interview them. To gather evidence on their behalf.' Jamie watches you. He is almost slavering, like a dog anticipating food.

'I don't know,' you say, wringing your hands.

'But don't you see, Irena? The more the world hears about what is happening...'

You snap, 'I know that.'

If my bleeding does not come soon, what will I do? This world is no place for my child to be born.

In the end, you agree. This earns you better food, an occasional shower. You give some of the food to Tikja.

People tell you of murders, rapes, houses burned, possessions stolen. And every time, it makes you remember. As if that were not enough, afterwards Jamie wears you down, coaxing, 'Tell us your own story, Irena,' he says.

You stand by the perimeter fence. Outside, beyond those hills, is Miran and home.

You say, 'I may be free, but I feel like a prisoner.'

Jamie stares at you. You feel his mind working.

'You see me as your jailer?'

'I didn't say that.'

You fidget, look everywhere; see no way to escape. 'Okay,' you say. 'I will talk.'

Although it is brief, you do not miss his smile of triumph.

You speak in monotone, separate yourself. It makes it easier to release the words but you still flinch when the question comes.

Jacqueline asks it very softly, but her eyes are like flint.

Once more you feel the chill of fear creep through your clothes, bite into your skin as your neighbour, Teodor, who Miran said would protect you, laughs at your screams when the soldiers drag you away. You tell all this to the woman Jacqueline.

Jacqueline's pen shakes.

And Jamie looks at you differently now. He rushes outside.

'Jamie!' Jacqueline's eyes are blazing. She follows him.

You hear her voice, raised. Jamie's, muffled. You sit, biting your nails.

Jacqueline and Jamie return.

'Where did they take you?' Jacqueline asks.

'To a town. Not just me, all the women. They shut us in houses.'

'Imprisoned you?'

'Three days. On the third, they...' Your tongue stumbles over the words.

Jacqueline gives you water. You sip slowly. You feel torpid. You open your mouth, speak, syllables catch in your throat.

'We can stop if you want.' Jacqueline's eyes seem warmer. She puts down her clipboard.

'No! No, it must be now.' You breathe deeply, take more water then you tell them about the question: Where is your husband? How they asked it over and over again until you no longer heard the words.

Your heart almost stops. Jacqueline scribbles furiously.

'Then there was the music.' You begin to cry.

Jacqueline says, 'That's enough,' but you shake your head.

Jamie's face is flushed. You glare at him, see him flinch. Jacqueline frowns but says nothing.

Your eyes sear Jamie's. 'They make me dance to it, strip. One by one, they come up. Touch.'

Jamie's eyes drop to your breasts. He licks his lips. A bead of sweat trickles down his brow. 'And then?' he says.

'Nothing. They said, 'Get dressed, you whore.''

Men are to be released from prison. Someone heard it on a radio. Expectation spreads through the camp. You know, but can't explain why, that Miran will be among them.

Jamie comes to see you.

'Go away, Jamie, it's done.'

'Why did you lie?' His voice is trembling.

'Who says I did?'

He reddens, gazes at his feet. 'They didn't just let you go, did they?'

'No.'

Jamie looks up, nods. His face turns paler. 'I've news,' he says. 'Two coaches will cross the border this afternoon.'

You run towards a tall man. He looks older, you think, thinner. His beard is rough, his clothes ragged but his bright eyes and the way he bears himself make him look like a king.

'Miran!'

He stumbles, shrugs you aside when you try to help but you do not mind. He was always a proud man. You feel as if the world has suddenly been set right. Now Miran is here nothing can go wrong again. And last night, you started bleeding.

You are given a tent of your own. You collect wild flowers, arrange them in a borrowed vase. Jacqueline lends some make-up, says you look pretty. You want this day to be perfect but Miran is annoyed because you bleed.

Jacqueline comes to see you settled. She says, 'Jamie is leaving.'

Miran's brow lifts. 'Who is Jamie?' he asks when Jacqueline has gone.

'A care worker.'

You see the judgement in Miran's eyes. He gets up, scowling. 'I want to walk.'

You smile and say you'll join him but he presses a forbidding hand on your shoulder.

'I meant alone.'

He is missing for hours. When he returns, his face is dark. 'I met some old neighbours,' he says.

'Miran says I am no longer his wife.'

The words are simple but the pain within them is worse than any you have known. Jacqueline finds you a place in another tent, among women you do not know.

You sit on your new bed, rock slowly to and fro. See no pictures, hear no words.

'Jacqueline told me,' Jamie says.

You look at him, see only a stranger. You are cold inside. Numb. 'Why are you here?'

'I feel responsible.'

'You weren't the one who told him.'

'I have abused you too.'

'That doesn't matter.'

'It matters to me.' Jamie twists and untwists his hands repeatedly. 'Why is Miran reacting like this?'

'He will be ridiculed if he keeps me.'

Jamie's eyes flash. 'Keeps you? What does he think you are, a pet kitten?'

'Miran is proud.'

Jamie is silent for a while then he says, 'I leave next week.'

You do not respond.

'I want you to come with me.'

'Jamie, go home. Forget me.'

He walks away, comes back, grabs you by the wrists.

'Jamie, you are hurting me!'

He drags you outside while the other women cower at the back of the tent.

You find Miran close to where you said you felt like a prisoner. Now you know you are one.

Miran sneers at Jamie, speaks in English. 'I thought you might turn up.' He doesn't look at you at all.

You wish you could sink into the ground.

Jamie's face is red, angry. 'They've taken everything else you had,' he shouts at Miran. 'Are you going to give them your marriage as well?'

Miran's eyes are full of contempt. You know that look so well.

'You wouldn't understand,' he says. 'She is unclean.' He pauses. 'Perhaps she gave herself to you too.'

You reach him first. Screaming, you pound your fists against Miran's chest. He flings you aside as if you were a piece of nothing then Jamie punches him, rocks him against the fence.

'You great long streak of piss,' Jamie shouts, his eyes afire. 'Believing that you were alive was all that kept Irena going. You desert her now and all her suffering, yours too, will have been for nothing.'

This new aspect of Jamie is impressive. You don't understand all his words but you want to share in them, make them change Miran's mind. Miran, however, says nothing. He pushes himself away from the fence.

Jamie shakes him violently, bawls into Miran's impassive face. 'Say something, you pillar of shit.'

Still Miran is silent.

Jamie sighs loudly and releases Miran, who spits on the ground then strides away with never a glance at you.

Jamie clings to the fence, looks up towards the mountains, his whole body shaking.

Jamie's bus pulls in. You reach up, touch him on the cheek.

'I'll miss you,' he says. His eyes are moist.

'I'll miss you too.'

'What will you do?'

'Go home when the killing stops. What else can I do?' You think of broken walls, roofs open to the sky, and how Miran twice walked away from you.

You let Jamie draw you into his arms, kiss you like a woman should be kissed.

'Irena, come with me instead,' he whispers, and for a long, long moment you picture a safe, neat house in his native land, though he has never said where that is.

You reach up, kiss him back, try not to look at his eyes.

Eamon Bunion's Christmas Cracker
(a tribute to Damon Runyon)

Now one time it comes on Christmas and in fact is three days before. I am in Smoking Jack's Breakfast Parlor on West Forty-seventh Street eating a Smoking Jack's Special which it is my custom to have at this hour, along towards eleven o'clock. Now, Smoking Jack's Specials are very popular in this neighbourhood and it is indeed a dish that sets a guy up for the day. I am taking my first mouthful when along comes a skinny guy I do not see around before.

He is different from the guys that usually frequent Smoking Jack's, because this one comes packaged as a priest. This makes me somewhat nervous as priest guys are inclined to seek donations in this season of goodwill. Now I wish to say I am as Christian as anyone, apart from this priest guy of course, but in these hard times I am averse to coughing up bucks. So I try to look inconspicuous which is difficult when I am the only customer despite Smoking Jack's Specials being so popular. Smoking Jack himself is missing too, as I see him duck below the counter as soon as he clocks the black shirt walking through the door.

The priest guy sits down at my table without so much as a by your leave. He says, 'I am Father Patrick O'Donnell, the curate at St Enigma's, and my boss Father Francis Bourke sends his compliments to Mister O'Flaherty.'

I start to say I am unacquainted with this O'Flaherty party but it is then that Smoking Jack puts his head above the counter and in fact comes over to my table and says, 'I am Mister O'Flaherty, the owner of this joint. I mistake you for a guy who runs with Herbie the Hammer, a fine citizen to whom I happen to owe a few Gs, which is the reason I am unable to contribute towards the good work of the parish.'

I understand now why Smoking Jack hides, because Herbie the Hammer is a guy you must not monkey with in any respect. In fact, he is a guy who blows your brains out at the slightest whim and I am glad I am not owing him any Gs.

'I do not want money,' says Father Patrick O'Donnell, 'but I am directing St Enigma's Nativity Play and we need a crib for the Heavenly Babe. Father Francis Bourke says you have suitable boxes.'

'This is indeed true,' says Smoking Jack, beaming like an oversized cherub. 'And it is my pleasure to donate one for the good of St Enigma.'

Smoking Jack leads us out back and there indeed are the boxes that Father Francis Bourke observes.

Father O'Donnell selects a nice clean one. 'Most appropriate,' he says, pointing at its side and I see that one time someone stamps 'Produce of Israel' into the wood.

I catch his point at once. Smoking Jack is somewhat slower.

Now, this box is a well-built job and, with Father Patrick O'Donnell being such a skinny guy, Smoking Jack and I carry it for him.

St Enigma's church hall is at the bottom of a dark alley. It is the kind of place where a guy only feels safe with a Roscoe in his hand, so Smoking Jack and I let Father Patrick O'Donnell go ahead first in case any hoodlum looking for an easy Christmas present thinks he might get lucky.

'Is that my crib?' comes a voice from behind.

Smoking Jack and I wheel around and see a doll of about twenty who looks sweeter than a million bucks. She is tall and dark, with curves that make a man weak at the knees.

Smoking Jack says, 'This crib is for you?' in a croaky kind of voice.

'Yes,' says the doll and smiles a smile that makes me think she is cuter than any doll I ever see before.

Smoking Jack comes over all daffy, crosses himself three times. 'You are a heavenly babe indeed,' he says.

'I bet you say that to every girl on Broadway,' says the heavenly babe, but she looks a look that says Smoking Jack is a cute guy. Now, this is a view with which I cannot concur, as personally I think he looks worse than the morning after a hard night with a couple bottles of dodgy Jack Daniels.

Father Patrick O'Donnell coughs loudly and says, 'This is my ever-loving sister Miss Mary O'Donnell, and she plays not the Heavenly Babe but the Virgin Mary herself.'

'The Virgin Mary herself,' echoes Smoking Jack, crossing himself again. His eyes fix firmly on Miss Mary O'Donnell's splendid chest as he says, 'Maybe I can play the Heavenly Babe.'

Miss Mary O'Donnell laughs ha-ha and turns to me, clocking me with coal-black eyes. 'And I suppose you want to play the Holy Ghost?'

I catch her drift and smile a smile that tells her so. And later we give Smoking Jack the slip and I escort Miss Mary O'Donnell to the Blue Lagoon on West Forty-ninth Street. It is then I learn she is not inhibited at all and in fact is a dancer there and does a hot routine wearing an ostrich feather and very little else besides.

She also tells me, 'I do not want to be the Virgin Mary at all but am persuaded to by my ever-loving brother.'

It seems the original Virgin is a judy with the handle Miss Anthea Drawbridge, and it is by no means a betrayal of confidence to tell you she looks similar to the nag that pulls Solly Simpson's beer cart.

It happens that in the first rehearsal, St Joseph, a guy by the name of Lenny Cappella, takes one look at the Virgin and does a nosedive through the window. Father Patrick O'Donnell follows him and it appears he is not such a weedy guy as he looks, because he hooks Lenny in a half nelson and marches him back to St Enigma's. However, Lenny is adamant he will not play St Joseph unless the current Virgin is given the boot.

It is then that Miss Mary O'Donnell comes seeking the bright lights of Broadway. Now, a part on Broadway is harder to find than a landlord's heart and so Miss Mary O'Donnell has to take the night job at the Blue Lagoon.

'Good,' says Father Patrick O'Donnell, 'then your afternoons are free. You shall be the Virgin in my nativity play, good practice for when you are setting the footlights on fire.'

So Miss Mary O'Donnell takes the part and Lenny Cappella is more than happy. However, it seems that Lenny has breath like a badger and Miss Mary O'Donnell reels every time he comes closer than a furlong, which is the reason why she does not want to be the Virgin Mary and only does it to please her ever-loving brother.

On the day for the nativity play, Smoking Jack and I escort Miss Mary O'Donnell to the stage door, which is in fact the back one, next to the trash.

There, Smoking Jack clocks St Joseph and says, 'Hey, this guy cannot play St Joseph. He is Leonard Chappell, a Southern Baptist, not a Catholic boy at all.'

'You stupid jerk,' says Lenny, who it seems changes his name to make folks think he runs with the Italian mobs. 'We have Joseph and the Virgin Mary just the same as you.'

Smoking Jack whistles like the Wabash Cannonball. 'Well, knock me down singing,' he says. 'I never hear tell of that.'

We settle down to the Heavenly Choir performing 'While shepherds watch their flocks by night'. Now, this Heavenly Choir happens to be a bunch of senior girls from St Nubila's Convent School, and I am bound to admit they bring tears to my eyes. Though whether through their fine sopranos or the fact they wear very short skirts and fishnet stockings I am hard put to say. When they finish, the Angel of the Lord appears. Miss Anthea Drawbridge is now the Angel instead of the Virgin, who is now of course Miss Mary O'Donnell.

Even though she plays the Angel, Miss Anthea Drawbridge still looks like a sackful of something the dog leaves on the step, but at least she has a thunderous voice, which is good for the part of the Angel of the Lord. She booms, 'Fear not,' and the Shepherds run for cover behind the sheep.

In the next scene, the Angel announces to the Virgin, 'Blessed art thou among women,' then, in a whispering thunderclap that is heard by the whole audience, she adds, 'You double-crossing two-bit floozy.'

The Virgin Mary is understandably upset by this hostility and messes up her next line somewhat. I hold my breath for I most definitely do not wish Miss Mary O'Donnell to come to any harm and Miss Anthea Drawbridge looks more terrifying than Herbie the Hammer himself. However, my action is unnecessary because the Angel merely smirks then shimmies off stage.

The scene shifts to the stable. Inside, the Virgin Mary and St Joseph sit with the cradle and a donkey and wait for the Shepherds and Three Kings. They wait longer than somewhat because a fight begins outside. How it starts is that King Balthazar calls one of the Shepherds a poof. Now this is unfortunate because this Shepherd boxes in the Golden Gloves and he biffs King Balthazar good and hard on the beezer and soon this Balthazar is looking like a client of Herbie the Hammer that Smoking Jack owes the Gs to.

The Angel appears, flexing her biceps. Personally, I prefer judies with less muscle and a lot less lip. The Shepherds deem it a wise moment to pay their respects to the Heavenly Babe.

After the Shepherds leave, the Three Kings come in with gold, frankincense and myrrh. The gold is a solid gold tray from the Five and Dime and the gold already flakes off. The frankincense is that skunk-smelling scent that drug stores peddle on Christmas Eve to guys who forget to buy their wives a present. The myrrh is a Cut-and-Come-Again cake the nuns bake for Father Patrick O'Donnell's recent birthday, and which the good Father gladly donates to the nativity play.

Throughout these proceedings, I see the Virgin Mary try hard to keep her face turned away from St Joseph. Luckily, the holy crib stands between them, decorated with tinsel and the ostrich feather that Miss Mary O'Donnell uses to such good effect at the Blue Lagoon.

Things seem to be proceeding to a merciful end but then, as the cast is leaving the stage, something snaps up above and everyone is rushing to avoid the falling Star of Bethlehem. In the confusion, the front half of the donkey turns left as its rear turns right and the beast splits in two, its back end emitting the sort of language which I personally feel is unfitting to be heard on religious premises.

Then Father Patrick O'Donnell appears with a collection box, which procedure empties the hall faster than a runaway moose, leaving only Smoking Jack and me.

Father Patrick O'Donnell shakes the collection box at us more vigorously than somewhat. I put in two bucks and Smoking Jack donates a lousy dime.

'Bless you, my sons,' says Father Patrick O'Donnell. 'May St Enigma intercede in your prayers.'

Then Miss Mary O'Donnell is there, cuter than ever, all in white, with spangled hair and a smile as big as Brooklyn. 'Merry Christmas, Patrick,' she says to her ever-loving brother, then links her arms in mine and Smoking Jack's. 'Now which of you two fine boys is escorting me home?'

Smoking Jack and I circle each other like fighting cats then walk Miss Mary O'Donnell towards West Forty-seventh Street. I am praying hard I get rid of Smoking Jack as soon as maybe. Sooner even.

As we pass Smoking Jack's Breakfast Parlor, a skinny guy in black comes out the doorway.

Smoking Jack says, 'Oh shit!'

Now, normally I am averse to uncouth expressions in the presence of a lady but this time I think maybe St Enigma deals me a winning hand.

The skinny guy indicates I better get lost, a request with which I am glad to comply on account of the Roscoe he holds in his duke. Personally, I am not inclined to hang around if someone points a Roscoe at me.

The guy then removes his hat and says to Miss Mary O'Donnell, as polite as you could wish, 'Excuse me, there is urgent business I wish to discuss with Mr O'Flaherty.'

He and Smoking Jack head for Smoking Jack's Breakfast Parlor and I guess Smoking Jack soon opens round the clock to replace the Gs that Herbie the Hammer's runner collects.

This interceding racket has possibilities, I am thinking. Maybe I soon go to church more often, negotiate a percentage with St Enigma.

Miss Mary O'Donnell says, 'Well, honey, I guess that just leaves you and me.' She giggles a giggle and snuggles up close as we walk on.

White Bikini Bottoms, Maroon Slippers

The wind was still blowing a hooley. Jim furled *Ondine*'s jib until only a tiny slab of white sail remained. Its triangular shape made him think of Mel's bikini bottoms, made him wish he could see her in the bikini now. Only Mel of course wasn't here, wasn't stuck in this tiny boat weathering a storm in the middle of Port Phillip Bay.

If he had listened to her, they might be strolling together right now along St Kilda Pier, en route to a lazy lunch at Little Blue. Then, if the sun managed to stop sulking, down to that sheltered section where the all-year swimmers congregated, men and women with hides as dark as Mel's brown mare.

'Too rough for you on the Bay today,' the wags at the marina had said, spinning 'you' out with long grins and old salts' nods.

'No worries,' Jim had responded, a stupid thing to say, he reflected now, on the day he might well drown.

Brooding clouds curled overhead. Unleashed iron squalls shot gunmetal waves houses high across the water. The white horses of earlier hours had turned to spindrift. Their spray lashed Jim's face, gnawed every worry line as he prayed against getting caught in the shipping lanes, prayed that any professional skippers about had decided safety lay in staying out at sea.

He weighed his chances of avoiding the Heads. Driven there, he'd have the rip as well as this gale to fight. He hoped the designer's assertions that *Ondine* was unsinkable were tested fact and not adman's hyperbole.

It seemed like fate had been against him from the start. Almost as soon as he was out of the marina, well before where he usually hoisted the sails, the outboard packed in and refused to restart. No use trying the damn thing now anyway; the prop would be out of the water a hundred times more than in it. He wished *Ondine* was more matron than water nymph, wished she had an inboard diesel, wished he had a marine radio instead of a mobile that couldn't find a signal. He wished a lot of other things.

Earlier, a freak gust ripped across *Ondine*'s beam, funnelled into fury through the gap between Mount Martha and Arthur's Seat. Jim still had the mainsail up then and hung on to the mainsheet a fraction too long.

'Let it go,' screamed a voice in his head and he let the boom swing out to spill the wind. *Ondine* spun almost a hundred and eighty degrees, began close-reaching on a starboard tack. Then the wind gusted again but this time when Jim tried to counter it, the mainsheet caught on something at the boat's stern, causing *Ondine* to broach violently, almost knocking her down.

Somehow, he'd scrabbled to the mast, brought the mainsail down, then aft to the cockpit to furl the jib to bikini bottom stage. That kept *Ondine* approximately stable while he decided what to do next. That step, at the moment, was a process bent on eluding him. The argument with Mel, on the other hand, refused to leave him alone.

The worst thing was it had been over nothing really. They'd been riding back from the city on the tram and in Swanston Street a grizzled old guy got on, stayed near the doors, ignored the ticket machine. It was obvious he didn't have a Metcard or Myki to validate, had no intention of buying either. His clothes looked as if they'd seen a few op shops too many but even so, in an ancient tweed overcoat about three sizes too large, dilapidated homburg hat overhead, maroon slippers on his feet, he was overdressed for that warm spring day. He also stank like a shed full of possums.

Jim, though three rows back from where the man stood, gagged at the smell. Standing passengers in closer range shuffled away, crowding each other so the offender gained a sizeable reserved space of his own.

He got off a few stops later but the tram did not start right away and Jim saw him rifle through an adjacent litter bin. Dipping deep, the man drew something out only to drop it on the ground, look down at it then glare at the litter bin as if that was somehow the cause of his loss. As the tram moved off, he shifted his gaze to Jim's window, stared vacantly through thick-lensed spectacles Jim suspected had never been prescribed for him.

'Poor beggar,' Mel said.

Jim, before he could restrain himself, said, 'Jeez,' shook his head.

'What?' Mel said.

Jim watched her eyes bead but he still went ahead and voiced his opinion. 'Bloody freeloading dero,' he said. 'What's the point of charging fares if nobody's around to check who's paid?'

'You don't know what shit he's had to face in his life,' Mel snapped. 'Try putting yourself in his shoes.'

'Slippers actually,' Jim said. 'Not shoes.'

That was the start and it didn't get any better. Jim spent the night alone on the fold-out couch.

With his mind chained to Mel, Jim's body was forced to function on autopilot. He was vaguely aware of it hunkering him on the windward side of the cockpit, clipping his safety harness to the pushpit rail and making his hand hold the tiller so the wind might fill the bikini and *Ondine* thus become compliant.

Although the waves remained tree-tall and she heeled constantly, *Ondine*'s yawing at last eased and she showed signs of accepting the course Jim's body had set. His hands allowed themselves to grip the tiller and jib sheet less desperately.

As Jim relived the reasons behind being stupid enough to be out here on a stormy Sunday, his eyes hovered between open and closed. Devoid of anything resembling sleep, long before dawn he'd risen, slurped down a few Weetbix, nibbled a piece of toast, and wondered what to do about Mel. It was then he'd registered the faint snores coming from behind the emphatically closed bedroom door.

'Seems she's had no bloody trouble sleeping,' he'd muttered and that belief magnified into a knot of defiance, though whether through resentment, jealousy or something more malevolent he was still hard put to say.

The last three Sundays they'd spent mostly on horseback up at Mel's parents' place near Ballarat, but yesterday, before their spat, he'd tried to talk her into sailing today instead. She'd hummed and hawed, said the forecast wasn't good and why didn't they sleep in late and then see. 'See' was Mel's shorthand for possible sex.

'We won't damn well see now, will we?' he'd yelled at the bedroom door that morning. Then he'd grabbed coat and keys, stormed out of the flat, slammed the front door shut behind him.

Muttering 'St Kilda, fuck every inch of you' as a one-line mantra approximating the tune to Johnny Cash's 'San Quentin', he'd run to the marina, a kilometre or so, arrived chest heaving. Within thirty minutes, still half breathless, after retrieving oilskins and outboard from the cabin, he was motoring *Ondine* out of her berth. Inside another half hour, the engine had cut out and the skies began to glower.

Jim shivered. What had begun to glower? No, the reminiscence was gone. He realised he'd dozed off. He shivered again, felt curiously lighter. The unbearable lightness of being flitted through his head, and for a moment he felt clever for dreaming such a phrase up. Then he recalled it was the title of a book he'd read. By Milan Kundera. And he was thus restored to reality. For the first time in he didn't know how many hours, he became fully aware of the sea, the weather, how *Ondine* was coping with it.

It seemed he'd managed to turn her about and she was now heading north-west. Four or five kilometres off the port beam he could see what surely must be Portarlington. By his reckoning, the wind had more south than east in it now. *Ondine* was certainly riding more steadily in the swell and the Heads were way, way astern.

Time to head home. In the top half of the Bay, he reassured himself, conditions were often better. He'd try some mainsail, turn that bikini bottom into something less scanty. Closer to St Kilda, he'd check the outboard. Probably dirt in the fuel line, easy enough to fix.

He tried to rise, had to sit down again; energy had apparently deserted him. He felt decidedly flimsy now, not just light, and recognised it as no ethereal mind state but the bonk, hunger knock, that could only be assuaged by food. He'd eaten nothing since breakfast, not drunk anything either unless you counted rain and sea spray.

He secured *Ondine*'s tiller with bungee cord, slid off the cockpit seat and through the companionway. In the cabin, his feet met two, three inches of water. Although he knew it could only be salt water, he still dipped a finger in to check. Must have poured in from the cockpit during the worst of the storm. Well, pumping it out would have to wait.

He flopped onto the port settee, glanced at the sodden Quaysiders on his feet. 'Put yourself in his shoes,' Mel had said. The tramp's slippers had been holed in places. And they were maroon. Symbolising the guy's life, Jim mused. Holed in too many places, marooned in a city where he didn't belong.

A bit like me. This revelation surprised him. Forget the bloody tramp, he told himself, you need food, quick. Last time he and Mel sailed, there'd been fruit and nut chocolate and he was pretty sure they hadn't eaten it all. And there was always coffee and fresh water in the container beneath the sink. Cold coffee would have to do; he didn't fancy boiling water in this sea.

He slid forward along the settee to the galley, discovered some plain biscuits as well as three pieces of chocolate. There was even a carton of skimmed milk, unopened. He opted for that rather than coffee.

For the first time that day, he felt lucky. His feet might be wet but the rest of him was dry enough, thanks to the oilskins. There were rubber boots in a cabin locker but it was a bit late to use them now.

With the mainsail double-reefed, Jim set course for home. The wind was almost directly behind him, so he'd need to keep a sharp eye for sudden shifts.

He wondered what Mel was doing with her Sunday, how pissed off with him she was. Maybe he should call her, but what could he say? 'Sorry' was a hard word and he didn't feel sorry, not for having an opinion.

He fished beneath his oilskins, brought out his mobile anyway, switched it on. Still no signal. He was about to put it away when it suddenly beeped to say he had a text message. No, two messages. They were both from Mel, obviously sent earlier while he was still in range, albeit with his phone switched off. The first said Please tell me you're not on that bloody boat. The second was Oh God, you are. Jim, sweetheart, come HOME.

Jim reread both messages, smiled, and at that precise moment, *Ondine* rocked as a gust arrived from the wrong direction. He had only seconds until the boom swung across the cockpit like a Louisville Slugger. Somehow, in one seamless movement, he dropped the mobile, ducked below the boom and, still holding the tiller, grabbed the mainsheet, regained control.

He felt himself shaking afterwards but the worst of it was in his mind. He should have been watching the wind. What if he'd been knocked unconscious, propelled overboard, even both? Sheesh, he'd read enough accounts of yachtsmen killed by booms striking them. And if you survived that bit and reached the water alive but unconscious, life jackets didn't always face you the right way up. Even if you didn't drown, what if you ended up brain-damaged, a half vegetable like – Jim hated to think this – like that guy on the tram?

Put yourself in his shoes. Maybe the guy was a Vietnam veteran, a hero, mind addled by the horrors he'd witnessed, been forced to take part in. Came back to find his country had disowned him, could only get menial work, took solace in drink, drugs, didn't matter which. End result the same: shuffling on and off Melbourne trams, getting nowhere day by day. Or perhaps he'd been born with an off-kilter brain, jeered at by other kids, shoved into a so-called training centre, kicked onto the streets when the funding stopped.

This poor bloke wouldn't even understand what an ordinary tram ticket was, so what chance would he have with the fucking Myki system? Mel was right, Jim thought. Except they were slippers, not shoes. And 'Sorry' isn't so hard to say, not if you really mean it.

Keeping one hand firmly on the tiller, he picked his mobile up, saw the signal bars climb.

He felt light again but it couldn't be hunger knock this time. Maybe it was the weight leaving his conscience.

Finding Indigo

29 August 1944

Travis Hollingfield, wearing his all-American smile, parades his Sherman tank through the streets of Paris. He thinks of Omaha Beach, of crossing Normandy hedgerow by bloody hedgerow, recalls this is his third Sherman in as many months. And God knows – he tries to bite this new thought back but like a door-to-door evangelist it keeps on coming – God knows how many lives it has all cost. Something dampens his eyes but he sets his jaw so that the smile lingers on.

The sidewalks are streaming with gay monsieurs and gayer mademoiselles. Reds, whites and blues of *le Tricouleur* and an occasional Stars and Stripes flow from opened windows and wave from the hands of the crowd. Rainbow strings of bunting stretch from lamp post to lamp post. Travis can make out all their component colours except indigo. He reflects that he's never been able to capture that – each time he's thought he had, it's turned tail on him and become mere violet, purple, or even blue. Still, indigo symbolises things as elusive as itself, things he doubts he'll ever find: spiritual realisation, wisdom. No wonder then that he can't see the goddamn colour.

'*Chocolat*, mister?' A snub-nosed boy breaks Travis's thoughts. He is running alongside the tank, looks up at Travis with dark, excited eyes. 'Hershey Bar,' he cries. 'Oncle Sam, we love you.' He's about the size of Travis's six-year-old son, but his pinched urchin face looks far older.

Travis grins at him then searches in a pocket. He finds an unused pack of chewing gum. 'Sorry, no Hershey Bars today.'

He throws the gum to the boy, who catches it in one hand then stands motionless, gazing at the wrapper while his lips form silent words.

In a tiny open square to his right, Travis notices a crowd surrounding a young woman. She, wearing a simple short-sleeved dress, is standing in the well of a horse-drawn cart. She doesn't look happy. Two burly men restrain her by the arms and the crowd don't seem bent on making friends with her either. Travis's grin disappears and his lips thin. He orders his driver to stop.

A third man, of scarecrow physique with clothes to match, climbs up into the cart. He extracts a pair of scissors from a tattered pocket and begins to hack at the woman's long dark hair. The crowd cheers and jeers and tomatoes begin to leave its ranks and hit the victim in the cart. They are large and the better aimed ones burst against her head and form rivulets down her cheeks. One or two fly past her and hit the man who's trying to shear her. Travis's grin returns for those.

He has the Sherman turn into the square, tells his driver to accelerate. Thirty-four tons of aggression part the crowd.

'What the fuck are you doing?' Travis bawls at the men in the cart.

They stare at Travis, then at the great grey barrel of gun pointing straight at them. The two holding the woman let go of her arms and the scarecrow drops the shears onto his feet.

'*Putain de merde*,' he says.

'I should damn well think so,' says Travis. He causes his Sherman to pull up alongside the cart and he scoops the woman up and out of it, sits her on top of his turret.

'Guess we better get you out of here,' he says and she gives him a scared little smile that cuts into his heart. Her eyes are haunted and haunting, their irises green.

Travis tells his driver to rev the engine hard to rescatter the crowd. The Sherman returns to the street of many colours but as it turns broadside to the square, a small object zooms out of the now sullen mass and shatters against the tank's right flank.

Travis looks down and sees a splat of yellow slap bang in the middle of the white star. Only powder paint, he decides, no sweat, it'll clean off later. He stops the tank for a moment and gives the crowd a thumbs-up. 'Good choice,' he shouts. 'Matches the stripes on your backs.'

The Sherman, back on its scheduled route, rumbles past jubilant

Parisians but Travis soon notices that the sight of his passenger mutes their cheering to a murmur. He figures shearing women's heads must be a popular pastime. He also figures that the US Army won't welcome a riot caused by one of their tank commanders sheltering an enemy of the people they've just liberated.

He dives into the Sherman's bowels and retrieves his garrison cap, which he places on the woman's head so the offending scalp is covered. Anyway, he tells himself, it's only humane to cover the gouges the scissors made. 'What am I going to do with you?' he asks her as he adjusts the cap until its edges sit neatly above her ears.

She smiles and he notices some of her scared look has gone. Then she treats him to a shrug and a wry twist of mouth. 'I don't know,' she says.

Her voice is soft, with an accent that Travis finds uncomfortably endearing. He notices her pupils have dilated and her irises are now blue, instead of green. The colour must change with the light, he supposes – like chameleons, like his experiences with indigo.

'You speak English?' he says.

'*Un peu,*' she says. 'A little.'

'What is your name?'

'Adèle.'

'Adèle,' Travis rolls the name on his tongue. 'Adèle, can you tell me why they cut off your hair?'

She pats her head. 'Hair? *Cheveux?*'

Travis nods. 'Yeah. Why did they cut it?'

Adèle gazes downwards, sighs. The sigh goes on so long Travis wonders if she's trying for a record. Then she mumbles something he can't catch.

'Hey, mister!' It's the boy who asked him for a Hershey Bar. He's waving what looks like a woman's headscarf. 'Here, mister. For the lady.'

Adèle straightens herself. She smiles at the boy. '*Merci,*' she says to him and, to Travis, she shows a face that's saying 'Please.'

Travis stops the Sherman and accepts the scarf. Adèle returns Travis's cap, puts the scarf over her head and knots it under her chin. The scarf is woollen, woven in subdued autumnal shades. Above all, it's inconspicuous and Travis is happy that it will cover any immediate suspicion an observer might harbour. Now he can concentrate on finding somewhere he can safely leave her. He sure as hell can't take her where his battalion's billeting for the night.

He checks his watch then throws his garrison cap to the boy, who puts it on his head at a jaunty angle and treats Travis to a smart salute. Travis knows the boy is hoping to hitch a ride. 'Sorry, son,' he says, pulling a face as he does, 'but we gotta go.'

'Okay, Oncle Sam.'

Travis bites his lip as he watches the boy waving, a rapidly diminishing figure as the Sherman accelerates away from him.

The radio crackles and his signals man pops his head into the cockpit area. 'For you, Trav,' he says.

Travis puts on his headphones and hears his company commander's voice.

'Where the hell are you, Travis? Leave those mademoiselles alone and get on up here. There's still plenty of war to fight. For us, starting five a.m. tomorrow.'

The Sherman picks up as much speed as Travis dares to let it have, given the density of the crowds but as the tank enters what seems to be a residential suburb, the onlookers diminish and keep on thinning the further it gets from the main thoroughfares. Travis zips the Sherman up to twenty-four miles per hour.

He notices the spires of a church looming ahead. As he nears it, he sees a priest walking across a large tree-lined square towards the church entrance. He orders his driver to turn into the square and pull up.

'Father, *Excusez-moi, s'il vous plaît.*' Travis is out of the Sherman and dashing towards the priest, who stops walking and waits for him.

Travis is breathing faster than he'd like. He summons up the remainder of his schoolboy French. '*Parlez-vous Anglais?*' he says.

The priest nods. 'Yes,' he says, smiling, or maybe even grinning. 'How can I help?'

Travis tells him how he came to have a passenger. He asks the priest why the crowd would shave her head.

'It's the punishment for sleeping with the enemy,' the priest says. 'Whether proven, suspected, or simply down to malice because the woman is beautiful.'

'Well, she is beautiful,' Travis says.

'*Eh bien, soit!*' the priest says then shrugs. 'Then she must be guilty.'

Together, he and Travis walk to the Sherman. Travis helps Adèle to the ground. The priest talks to her in rapid French. Adèle responds at a slower speed, accompanied by much frowning, lip chewing and hand wringing but gradually these movements become sparse and Travis even notices an occasional smile. He's no idea of what has been said, apart from '*Oui*' and '*Non*'.

The interrogation ends and the priest tells Travis, 'She has suffered enough. She will be safe with me.' He addresses Adèle again, who nods and turns to Travis.

'Thank you,' she says, then stretches up and kisses him on both cheeks.

Travis feels his face heating. Then Adèle's arms curl around him and somehow he finds his own responding in kind. If she did share a German's bed, he is certain she would not have done it lightly. She may have had a starving family to feed. Perhaps she was raped – it wouldn't be the first time the victim has been blamed for the crime. Or maybe she simply fell in love – that can be the hardest thing of all to bear.

He thinks of his wife back home in Oklahoma City, her blonde curls and her pale pink cashmere twinset. It's been a long, long time since he held a woman as close as this. For one long minute, he tightens his grip on Adèle. Then he sets her free. She smiles back at him and waves a hand as she walks away with the priest.

Ahead of Travis, a pale sun emerges from a cloud and its light filters through the canopies of the churchyard trees and brushes his face. As it does, he squeezes his eyes shut and the colour behind their lids is indigo.

Scorpio, Scorpio…

The emails began on the day my divorce became final: *Scorpio, Scorpio! Wherefore art thou, Scorpio?* The sender was Juliet Capulet.

Someone fooling around, I told myself, someone who knows my birth sign. Fionnuala? Not her style. My sister, my secretary? One doesn't know what email is; the other has no imagination.

I tapped in, *Wherefore art thou, Juliet?*

She replied within an hour: *Seek me here.*

I didn't know where to begin. I grabbed some chilled Michelobs, flopped in an armchair and emptied three bottles before I realised 'here' must mean the Internet.

A search produced over seven hundred contenders, mostly Shakespeare, with Prokofiev and Gounod running a long way behind. One site showed a girl seated, head resting on her upturned palm. There was nothing to identify her but I knew who she was, and the time and place: Maria Dancelli, 24 August 1978, Naples. I took the photograph on her seventeenth birthday.

I guessed she'd read about the affair. God knows, our press made enough noise. It must have reached the Italian papers too. I'll never forget the day I disturbed Fionnuala as she mounted her cabinet minister. It was the way she sneered that really hit me. That closed the file on our marriage. No kids to pay the price. In retrospect, it was just as well.

Maria loved children. I imagined her now: approaching forty, plump and jolly like her Mamma, ruling over a beautiful, olive-skinned brood. She knew I'd accessed her website. *See how she leans her cheek upon her hand. Oh that Scorpio might touch that cheek.*

Romeo and Juliet again, give or take a few words. I replied, *Maria, give me a phone number, an address. Meet me – anywhere you like. Please.*

I sleepwalked through the following day. All I could think of was Maria. Fionnuala, our marriage, our divorce, were relegated to oblivion.

I scanned my mail. A word nudged my memory and I leafed back through the papers. Naples! A client wanted a report on a company there.

My mind drifted back to Naples, 1978. I was finance director of my then employer's latest toy, a property company. It was a commercial disaster. Each track we took led to a one-way street with the *Camorra* waiting at the end.

I met Maria on the day I arrived. Her dark Latin eyes enchanted me and in cassette-course Italian, I invited her to dinner. That began our affair. We had to be circumspect; her father and brothers were *Camorristi* and she said, 'Peter, I don't want you dead in a gutter.' Although there was always an underlying hint of violence, I was never actually threatened. Her Mamma took to me and they didn't dare oppose her.

After seven months, I was recalled to London. Without bothering to warn me, my boss had sold out. I promised to return, but when Maria stopped answering my letters I was afraid to find out why. So that's that, I thought. *Et tu*, Maria.

I built up my own practice, working twenty hours a day, seven days a week. Two years later, I met Fionnuala – hard-nosed, hard-hearted and rich.

Maria must have left home years ago and I didn't fancy calling her papa. I thought of my old deputy, Gianni Punzi. He'd stayed under the new regime. Keeping my fingers crossed that the company still existed and he was still there, I called him.

It did and he was. Dottore Punzi now. 'Sure I remember Maria. Nice girl. No, Peter, she leaves soon after you. I do not see her since.'

'Would anyone know where she is now?'

'*Dio*! It's twenty years, Peter.'

Within twenty-four hours, he phoned back. 'You're in luck, my friend. My *segretaria*, you remember Gabriella? She and Maria exchange cards each Christmas. Maria moves to Verona. She remains Signorina Dancelli, by the way.'

Verona? Is that why she thought of Romeo and Juliet? And unmarried.

Apparently. That comforted me, though I'd be hard put to explain why. I wondered how she liked Verona. The Veronese looked down on *terrone* from the south. I'd been there a few times; it was beautiful, rich. Not like shabby old Naples at all. They could well have been in separate countries.

La Rondine, Paradise Street Centre, 2.30 Saturday. I wasn't expecting that. Had she really been in London all along? My nerves were as tight as a taxman's heart by Saturday and I spent the morning shuttling to and from the loo. Twenty years was one hell of a gap.

I parked beneath the Paradise Street Centre, took the lift to La Rondine. It was on the first floor but masquerading as a pavement café. Chain-sipping espressos, I looked out over the central well, scrutinising the shoppers below. Long before two-thirty came and went, I was a wreck.

A woman approached the escalator opposite. Slim, around five-eight, long black hair, enormous scarlet sunglasses. It looked like Maria, but I couldn't be certain. I stood up and she waved, slowly and deliberately. Her jacket swung open. Printed across the T-shirt underneath, in bright red, was *Ciao Scorpio*!

My heart must have passed one-ninety to the minute. She'd already reached the bottom of the escalator and was skipping off towards the exits. By the time I made the ground floor, she'd gone. I searched the bustling streets but I'd had the only glimpse of her she intended me to see that day.

Scorpio, be sure your sins have found you out. This had me wishing I was still taking Prozac. Maria had found me out and yes, damn her, I felt guilty. But if she wouldn't talk face to face… I logged off without replying and left her to figure out why.

Early, Tuesday evening, a car pulled up outside. The driver tooted the horn repeatedly and I looked out, annoyed. It was an Alfa Romeo, red, sleek, beautiful, a nineteen-sixties Giulietta Sprint – Romeo and Juliet again. And Maria – still hiding behind those bloody glasses. Before I could move, she blew a flamboyant kiss, let in the clutch and roared off like a boy racer.

Curiosity won over pig-headedness and I read my email: *Why dost thou not write? Dear Scorpio, if thou be honourable, send me word tonight.*

Honourable? I'd had enough of this. I hammered, *Up yours Juliet!* into the keyboard and sort solace with Irish malt in a glass and Angela Gheorghiu on the Marantz.

I was beginning to mellow when I heard a loud crack and my sitting room carpet became spattered with glass. A half-brick wrapped in paper lay in the middle of it.

It was another cryptic message: *What brick through yonder window breaks? You sought me here. Now seek me there. Farewell.* Shakespeare again, mostly. And the Scarlet Pimpernel.

She ignored my follow-up emails and in my head I began to see her everywhere. I'd pick her out among a crowd, stare at anyone who faintly resembled her until they turned away or stared me out in return. Once, I stalked a woman, sure that she was Maria. When she screamed, terrified, I almost screamed myself.

After two weeks, I received an envelope postmarked Verona. Inside was a copy of a P&O ferry ticket: Portsmouth to Cherbourg, dated the day after she threw the brick. So she'd driven home by the pretty route. I presumed the postmark was meant as a clue. She didn't know I already had her address.

She'd teased me long enough. I caught an Alitalia flight and, cramped up in my seat, closed my eyes and relived my last days with Maria.

We'd escaped Naples for Sorrento. Trying to forget what lay ahead, we enjoyed three nights together in a small hotel. On our last morning we strolled hand-in-hand up the Via del Capo and stood for an hour or more, gazing out over the bay towards Vesuvius and the dirty old city.

We said goodbye at Napoli Centrale.

I buried my face in Maria's hair. 'I love you,' I whispered then boarded my train while I still had the willpower.

Her face began to crumple as my train pulled out.

Now, I was in Italy again. After catching a bus from Catullo Airport, I registered at a city-centre hotel, trudged up to my room and fell asleep.

Next morning, I took a taxi to the sort of suburb where every other car is a BMW. I spotted the little Alfa as soon as we turned into Maria's road. I'd rehearsed what I was going to say, but it all went to pieces when she opened her door. She could easily have passed for ten years less than the thirty-seven I knew her to be. And she could never have guessed I'd find her so quickly. You could have heard her gasp three blocks away.

'*Dio*! It is really you?'

The house was furnished simply but elegantly. Maria, wearing a cream silk suit, complemented her surroundings well. I, in travel-weary chainstore grey, felt totally out of place.

She poured herself a large cognac. 'You?' Her hands were trembling.

'Please.' I felt shaky too. I gulped my brandy down and, before I could stop myself, said, 'Maria, you look lovely.'

'You are okay yourself.' It wasn't much, but I misread the signs and tried to kiss her. She shrugged me off violently. '*Per carità*! You think you just pick up where you leave off?' Her eyes were sparking.

'What happened, Maria? Why did you stop writing?'

She wouldn't look at me. Poured herself another drink. Didn't offer me one. 'It is for the best,' she said, tossing her hair back.

'How can you say that? How can you forget Sorrento?'

'Oh, I don't forget Sorrento. Don't worry about that. But you leave me, Peter. You leave me.' Her eyes were aflame now.

'You know I had no choice.'

'Always there is choice, Peter.'

'I wrote you endless letters, for Christ's sake.'

She screamed at me. '*Mannaggia*! What are letters? Nothing. I have no one to turn to. Nobody at all. Now you come twisting the knife. Why are you here, Peter? Why?' She paused for breath. Her eyes narrowed. 'Go away. Leave me alone.'

I didn't move. She glared at me then sat down.

We maintained a flinty silence for a lifetime then finally she tutted and said, 'Peter, why are you here?'

I knew I risked another blitz. 'Maria, you know why,' I said. It sounded patronising.

'Peter, I do not. Otherwise why do I ask?' She spat the last four words out.

'The emails. The Paradise Centre. Not to mention the brick.'

'Tchhh. I don't know what you talk about.'

'And I suppose that isn't your car outside?'

'What's that to do with it?' Delivered like a hail of tracer bullets.

'Do you deny sitting outside my house, blaring your horn?'

I watched her face clear then cloud over again.

'Stop it, both of you.'

I whipped round too quickly, nearly putting my neck out. Framed in a doorway was a younger Maria. She wore a white T-shirt with *Ciao Scorpio!* printed boldly across the chest.

Maria assaulted her in rapid Italian. I caught the gist: 'Giulietta, what the hell have you been up to?' Only she wasn't that polite.

Giulietta retaliated in the same way.

'Okay Peter, there's something you should know.'

I'd already worked it out. My mouth must have looked like the entrance to the Channel Tunnel. I looked at Giulietta and she looked back at me. Her eyes were sparkling, her face glowing.

'Maria, why didn't you tell me? And don't give me that shit again. Jesus, if I'd known, I would have come back at once.'

'*Stronzo di merde!*' Her face reddening more with each word, she hurled invective then burst into tears.

Giulietta began to cry too.

I don't know where I went, what I did, what I thought. The next thing I remember is walking into the lobby of my hotel two days later.

'Where have you been?' Giulietta sounded cross then she looked at me and grinned. 'Papa, you look like shit.'

Papa! She called me Papa. My mind was churning as she drove. Giulietta, Giulietta. All those years I missed. Your first steps; starting school; birthdays; holidays; tantrums; spots; boyfriends. The list was endless. By the time we reached Maria's, I'd stopped fighting the tears.

Maria was solemn-faced. 'So, you run away again, Peter.'

'Mamma! You promised.'

Maria looked warily at Giulietta then back at me. 'Okay. Is just as well you leave Napoli, Peter. My brothers wish to cut your throat. I am sent here to Verona. And I stay after Giulietta is born.'

'Didn't you ever marry?' I was jealous, although I had no right to be.

She shook her head. 'There are men of course. But always they want too much.' She snarled at me, 'I live and work for Giulietta only.'

Her eyes were brimming and Giulietta squeezed her hand. 'Mamma, it's because of me Papa is here. But it was you he came for, Mamma. I don't want to lose him again.'

'Hmmph.' Maria snorted, blew her nose and sat, lips pressed tightly together, staring at the wall.

Giulietta said, 'Mamma sees you in *La Repubblica*. She says, Giulietta, this man is your father. I was to start university, and I say, if I am now English, can I go to London. So, I begin at Kings College last year. Reading literature.'

'Shakespeare, by any chance?'

'You guessed of course.' Her smile was like I remembered Maria's. 'It wasn't so hard to find you – your institute tells me where you work.'

'I'm impressed.' She was a resourceful girl.

'I follow you, but you never notice. And I am shy of it. So I get this idea.' She smiled impishly. 'I will tease, make you think it is Mamma. I better not say who gives me your email address. Then I have this T-shirt, and think, that's it. I'm sorry about La Rondine. I lose my nerve. Then the same at your house.'

'What about my window?' I tried to growl but couldn't sustain it.

She pouted. 'You were mean to me.'

'So you sent a message I couldn't ignore?'

She nodded, grinned. 'I won't give our address, because of Mamma. I was going to try again next term.'

I'd noticed Maria's eyes open wider with each of Giulietta's words. Finally she spoke. 'I think you are very naughty girl, Giulietta. Maybe when you go back to London you stay with your father. That way you learn him and he keeps you in order. Save your Mamma from worrying.' She was still frozen-faced, but there was a hint of a thaw.

Giulietta's eyes were dancing. She flung her arms around Maria. 'Oh, Mamma, thank you Mamma.'

'Better ask your father first,' said Maria.

'May I, Papa?' Oh, that smile again.

I screwed my face up, said, 'Oh, I suppose so,' but my heart was leaping. I turned to Maria. 'Perhaps you would come too – a holiday?'

'Don't push your luck, Peter.'

I thought, at least I've gained a daughter. And maybe…

How long have you been sleeping with Freud?

My dad's name was Jack Pruitt and sixteen weeks and four days ago he fell from a cat-cracker at the oil refinery. The company's man in charge of bereavements called at the house and assured me Dad wouldn't have felt a thing. I nodded and said I understood, then he gave me a gold badge that Dad had been due to get. He said it was an award for long service.

After seeing the man out, I went upstairs and read Dad's love letters to Mum. She must have returned them after she left but he'd never opened the envelope. I found it, still sealed, in the bottom of the linen basket beneath his dirty clothes.

That evening saw me driving for the first time along the lane that I'm taking tonight. It's developed into a habit. It could take me right to the edge of the sea but I'm not travelling that far. Not yet.

Dark shapes loom up ahead, spectral, menacing in the pale moonlight. Then my headlights pick out a faded sign – Leastowe Ten is Club Me bers Only – and I turn in through an open gateway, park on a gravel area where the grass courts used to be. The spectral shapes are revealed as two old Nissen huts, bolted together and painted black, scarcely menacing at all. Above a steel-clad door a flickering sign declares Love-All. Beyond the huts are three hard courts with sagging nets and thistles sprouting through cracked asphalt.

A grill slides back to reveal the would-be-fifty-something who owns the place. Her face is shrivelled, nut-brown, and her name is Elsie. She holds out her hand for money – she always claims the membership is full, so I get to pay each time. I grunt my usual complaint and she gives her usual response: 'If you don't like it, don't come.'

And to think this was where I was conceived. I try to imagine the occasion – the lovers arrive on sit-up-and-beg bikes with wicker-basketed handlebars and racquets clamped to the forks. They play a few games then gaze at each other all daft and gooey-eyed before Dad serves for victory. It would have been on grass of course, perhaps in the exact spot where my car was standing.

I glance into the dance room – dim lights, a sickly shade of pink, and Status Quo being mangled by a band in the corner. Elsie claims the Beatles played here once, before 'Love me do', cost her all of thirty quid.

Apart from the band, things are quiet, just four girls dancing together. One waves. I wave back then go into the lounge, where the loudest sound is Hilly's laughter. She's a girl I went to school with. She makes room for me but my attention is focused on a dark-haired girl I haven't seen before. She's beautiful and she knows it.

'Who's she?' I nod towards the girl.

'Ann. Fancy your chances, Charlie?'

'No, just wondered who she was.'

I'm desperate to get Ann's attention, but everything I say is ignored. All the time, she's preening herself, gently shifting position on her stool so her little black dress rides ever so discreetly up her thighs. I begin to get annoyed. They're very nice thighs, but I'm anxiously seeking some flaw, something to take that look off her perfect face.

Finally the words spill out. 'Your lips are too thin.'

Ann's quiver and she looks as if she's about to burst into tears. There's an uneasy hush, and everyone looks away.

Joan, the girl who waved to me, is with me in my car. She's pretty enough, with neat blonde hair and soulful eyes I'm staring into.

Joan loses the soulful look and starts to frown. 'You look really odd, Charlie. What's the matter?'

'Got something on my mind.'

'But not me, though?' She pushes me away. 'No hard feelings tonight then, Charlie?' She chuckles at her joke, but it's high-pitched, edgy. She goes back to the club.

I stay in my car, rocking forwards, backwards in my seat. I haven't seen my mum for twenty years.

I'm back the following evening and Hilly greets me with a wicked smile. 'Joan reckons you're turning queer.'

'Got it wrong then, hasn't she?'

She shrugs. 'How should I know?'

I buy her a gin and tonic. 'Wouldn't you like to try me out?'

'Don't, Charlie.' Hilly sounds sorry for me. Then she gives me a curious look. 'Ann talked of nothing but you after you left. You really got under her skin. She could be your next.'

'Maybe I don't want her to be.'

A country and western band is playing.

Hilly grins, flutters her eyes. 'Old-fashioned music, Charlie. Let's dance.'

Soon we've had too much drink and we're swaying at dangerous angles.

Elsie tuts. 'One of you'd better take the other home.'

Hilly sticks her tongue out as we leave.

We sit in my car. We're petting but it doesn't seem right. I wonder if Hilly feels the same. I'm the first to stop and she sighs, strokes my forehead.

'You're a funny guy, Charlie.' She kisses her index finger and traces a line across my lips with it. 'Maybe we just got the timing wrong.'

Her touch feels like a kind of absolution and before I can stop myself, I'm telling her all about my dad, the letters, everything.

Hilly suddenly seems very sober. 'So when you're with a girl, you keep imagining she's your mother?'

'Hey, perhaps I'm trying to lay the ghost.' I start to laugh but it feels like I'm crying. 'Don't you think that's funny, Hilly?'

'No, I don't, Charlie.'

Hilly's silent for a long time, staring through the window. I look too, see it has started to rain.

Hilly brushes my cheek with her fingertips. 'Charlie, when you lose a parent…' She draws herself up until she's looking down at me. 'D'you really want to know what I think? Your father's death has brought the loss of your mother home to you – something you'd suppressed deep inside.'

'I was four years old when she walked out. Then they walled me up in a children's home. So you're damn right I suppressed it. Whingeing for Mummy didn't go down too well in Colditz.'

'Jesus, Charlie, I'm sorry. But my point is that you're trying to come to terms with two deaths, one physical one and one symbolic. So you end up looking for closure here, in the place where you began.'

'How long have you been sleeping with Freud?'

Hilly looks apologetic. 'I used to read a bit of psychology.'

'So tell me why I'm trying to screw my way through the club.'

She stares at me, unblinking. I've never noticed how tender her eyes can look.

'It's part of the same process, I suppose, recreating your conception. But I think you've already worked that out, Charlie.'

The drink seems to slide off me and I feel sober enough to drive Hilly home.

On the way she says, suddenly, 'Charlie, did you know I have a son?'

'A son?'

'Don't look so surprised.'

I'm seeing Hilly in a new light. 'What's his name?'

'Luke. He's three and a half.'

I must be wearing a stupid expression because she frowns. 'Charlie, stop it. I'm telling you this because he began life a bit like you.'

'What, at the tennis club?'

She laughs softly, it sounds like muted bells. 'I didn't mean that similar. Outside the rugby club actually – my very first time – one lousy fuck.' Her eyes are moist. 'You see, you're not unique.'

'Who's the father?'

'Just a boy. We were both drunk.'

Suddenly, I feel that I should have been the one. 'D'you still see him?'

'Charlie, I never even knew his name.'

Hilly pays her babysitter and invites me in for coffee. Luke is still awake and his face lights up when he sees me.

'Daddy!'

I wonder if he says that to every man who visits.

Hilly makes the coffee strong and black.

Luke climbs onto my lap and she tries to move him but I say, 'Let him stay.' I'm hoping he won't grow up obsessed about his father.

'I've been thinking,' Hilly says. 'Elsie might remember your parents. She's been at the club since the Stone Age, when they actually played tennis.'

Elsie raises her eyebrows. 'So you're Jack Pruitt's boy. And Sally Davis's. You should have said. I'd have offered you membership then.' She rummages through a drawer and passes me a photograph of young people dressed for tennis. Scrawled on the back is LTC August 1959, the year before I was born.

I've already recognised Dad and suddenly I remember the girl smiling shyly by his side. She, leaning over my cot, tucking me in, kissing me goodnight. My small figure walking beside her, my arm outstretched, holding her hand. Then another, later time when I reached for her, only to find that I was looking up at a stranger.

Elsie has trouble meeting my eyes. 'I'm sorry about the orphanage.'

I glare at Hilly, but she shakes her head and mouths, 'Not me.'

Elsie says, 'Jack couldn't cope. He was drinking heavily.'

'He managed to keep that up. What really happened? Why did my mother leave?'

Elsie breathes in deeply. 'Sally and her father were...very close. He used to interfere, give her money, things... Jack resented that. There were niggles, then full-scale rows and one night Jack gave Sally a beating and she left.'

'He swore she ran off with another man.'

Elsie turns her eyes away. 'No, there was no other man. Sally and her father emigrated to Canada. A fresh start, they said...'

'While I was incarcerated in that so-called Christian home.'

Elsie chews her bottom lip. 'She loved you, you know. She was heartbroken.'

'Then why did she let me go?' My fists are clenched tight.

'Sally was her father's daughter and he was a…persuasive man.' Elsie lowers her eyes.

'Forget it, Elsie. I think I've heard enough.'

Her face lightens and Hilly squeezes my hand.

I leave Hilly and Elsie together then sit in my car. I expect I'll feel better now that I know.

After an hour or so, there's a knock on my window.

It's Hilly. 'Someone to see you,' she says.

It's Ann of the thin lips. Hilly hurries away, head bowed, towards the clubhouse. I get out of the car, start to follow her.

'Charlie, it's cold. Can I get in?'

A nerve snatches in my temple and I turn around. I've forgotten Ann is there.

'It's the most hurtful thing anyone's ever said.'

Ann is tearful, asks me to take her home. I want to say no, but her eyes are begging me and I give in. Outside her door, she starts in on me, desperate to please but I can't even raise a smile. Instead, I tell her why I was so mean. I tell her she's beautiful and her lips are fine then I watch how quickly she can switch from desolation to victory. She pecks me goodnight and goes indoors.

I drive home, can't sleep, go out again and at half-past six I'm outside Hilly's flat, trying to work out what's bothering me. I glance up at her windows but there's no sign of her stirring. As a church bell chimes seven, I begin to cry over my dad, my mum, everything. Twenty years of grief and pain flood out. I cry for Hilly too. I want to hide myself in her arms.

A light comes on in the flat and I see Hilly draw back her curtains. She's hugging Luke to her chest and I recall how easily I let her walk away. Maybe I'm not too early, I think. Maybe I'm too late.

Hilly is looking out of her window. I don't know if she can see me in the morning gloom but I cross my fingers, breathe out as slowly as I can and begin the long walk towards her door.

What nil was it, mister?

1 September 2001

A newsflash comes over the radio – England 5, Germany 1.

Everyone shakes their heads like they don't believe it but their expressions say they want it to be true, so I guess Aussie rules doesn't rule Victoria, not absolutely. Someone says the announcer's got it wrong, it's surely the other way round. However, the score's not only confirmed but each England goal was scored by a Liverpool player, a hat trick for Owen, one each for Gerrard and Heskey.

I imagine being in a Liverpool pub at that moment. It would be bollocks to England; Liverpool 5, Germany 1.

Meg and I have driven from Ballarat for a sailing weekend in Mornington. This is the pre-regatta dinner. Football wasn't on the menu but now it has me hooked like I was still twenty years old. It's catching Meg too. I watch her eyes shine as she picks up on the excitement.

It's over thirty years since I saw Liverpool play live but that day carries baggage I still don't care to unpack.

7 January 1967

I set off early to make sure of a place in front of a barrier because Kop surges are breathtaking, permanently so on the wrong day.

I park well away from the ground but still have to hand protection money to the scallywag who asks, 'Mind yer car, mister?'

'You'll get the other half when I come back,' I growl.

He grins, knowing that I know the rules. I walk on to Anfield, certain that my car will be waiting, untouched, when I return.

Soon there's scarcely an inch to move and the only available air is scented with marijuana. A donkey-jacketed man rolls his Echo into a cylinder and pees through it onto a city suit in front. For all I know, someone's doing the same to me.

Gerry Marsden warbles through the Tannoys, 'You'll ne-e-ever walk alone.' The crowd adds 30,000 variations until the words and melody are barely recognisable. A low humming becomes a mighty roar as the mascot runs onto the pitch, followed by an army in red. It's a glorious sight, this Liverpool team. I and everyone on the Kop can recite the names like a sacred incantation: Lawrence, Lawler, Byrne, Strong, Yeats, Smith, Callaghan, Stevenson, St John, Hunt, Thompson. Repeatedly, we clap da-da, da-da-da, da-da-da, da then give an exultant, consolidated 'St John!' Ian St John waves, runs along the touchline, bounces a football from thigh to head and back again.

The visitors are cheered on. Claret and blue. The Hammers.

'Bobby Moore OBE!' the Kop chants.

Bobby grins and bows.

'Bobby Moore OBE. Other Buggers' Energy. Sir Roger Hunt! Sir Roger Hunt!'

Bobby's grin perishes but the Kop's undaunted. It sings, 'We're the best behaved supporters in the land.'

The game isn't the best I've seen, two nil to Liverpool at full time and I've already forgotten who scored the goals. Returning to the car, I take a shortcut through an area of two-up-two-downs and a boy looks up at me from a red-polished doorstep. He's four, five at a pinch, urchin face, knees scuffed. He wears threadbare flannel shorts, is sockless, and the canvas pumps on his feet are grey with age. A toe pokes out from the left one.

'What nil was it, mister?' he says.

I chuckle at his presumption. Inside, I'm wishing I could believe in something that much.

Back home, I join the usual crowd in the Crown.

'Oh, yer've won one, have yer?' growls the landlord.

The blue-and-white Everton rosettes pinned behind his bar become colourless, faded by our legion of red-and-white scarves.

1 September 2001

Those scarves meant you belonged, at least on match days, even if you reverted to nothing afterwards.

Our table today displays red and white too: crisp white tablecloth, red carnations in a white vase, red candle. In further homage, I order a noble red from Coonawarra. As Meg takes her first sip, I can see she's impressed. She gives me her raised-eyebrow nod.

'The match commentary is in five minutes,' the radio announces.

When it begins, all conversations stop. Six minutes from the start, Germany open the scoring. If this was live, we'd all be groaning but now we dismiss the adversity with a shrug.

As our soup arrives (leek and stilton), Gerrard loops a ball to Neville, who back-heads it to Barmby, who nods it to Owen, who fires it home to equalise. I wince as the soup scalds my tongue.

Gerrard drives the ball from twenty-five yards to score England's second goal and I cheer along with everyone else in the room. I order a second Coonawarra red.

Our euphoria rises with each retroactive goal. Three minutes into the second half, we're hysterical as Owen gets England's third.

We commiserate with the Germans on two near misses then almost shake the plaster from the ceiling as we applaud England's fourth, a cross from Gerrard to Owen who prods it into the net for his hat trick.

Our main course arrives: sizzling chateaubriand, wild mushrooms, béarnaise sauce. Heskey's goal, the fifth and last, coincides with our first mouthful. Meg says, 'Mmmwa' while I make eyes at her.

By the time the finer points of the match are being analysed, the wine's given me an AC/DC high-voltage glow. My face is lit like a politician's at election time.

Then I recall that kid on the doorstep…

7 January 1967

There was something about his face…

I finally realise who he reminds me of. I return to his criss-cross humble streets, mooch past disintegrating woodwork and crumbling mortar. Faces peer from the few windows that still retain glass. Children hog the street corner. No adults emerge, at least not through their front doors. I imagine them discussing me over backyard walls. 'Long streak of piss in a suit… Gotta be CID.'

When I was a kid, these streets scared me shitless. They're off a road I had to cycle along to school and I always imagined I was passing the jaws of hell. Once, a sharp crack echoed in the grimy terraces and something blew my back tyre out. I made that flat last another mile, pedalling like Anquetil himself to the safety of what passed for civilisation.

I can't decide which house it was but my persistence draws her out eventually. Heroin eyes accuse me from behind a fractionally opened door.

'How the hell did you find me? What do you want, Jonesy?'

'Saw little George outside, after the match. Didn't realise who he was until I got home. Wondered how you both were, if you needed help.'

She snorts. 'Help? Jesus, Mary and Joseph. Three years since I seen you and now you got the cheek to offer help. You're a joke, Jonesy.'

'Wouldn't have been three years if you'd told me you were moving.' I get my wallet out.

She hisses, 'Not here! Round the back.'

The door shrieks as it closes.

I push through street-corner kids, reach the back entry. Her gate's open. I enter a scullery that's damper than the yard outside. In full view, she's as scrawny as ever, same urchin face, same ratty hair.

I extract tenners from my wallet, watch her count them. 'Can I…?' I nod towards an archway, can see stairs beyond it.

'No. He's asleep. You think two hundred lousy quid and a conscience entitles you to access after all this time? Just piss off, Jonesy. Count yourself lucky.' Her chin's thrust forward, her eyes hard-glazed, two brown beads. She puts the money in one of those biscuit tins with a hinged lid, turns her back on me.

I return to the Crown, sink two pints without pausing, think about the day I met her. She was waiting for a bus outside a pub I rolled out of. I was seventeen, pissed and not feeling fussy. She said she had her own flat so when her bus arrived I scuttled on behind her.

We drank gin in a dingy club full of hollow faces that scared the shit out of me. I got to thinking this was a bad idea and it was best to get it over with and go. So as soon as we'd staggered to her flat, I slipped my hand up her skirt.

She pouted, 'Aren't you going to coax me?' She sounded as if she had tonsillitis.

I stroked her chest for a while, couldn't find anything there.

She started moaning, 'Oh baby, that feels nice. Don't stop.'

When I left, she said, 'You never told me your name.'

'George Jones,' I said, reading it from a poster in the window of a music shop next door.

Nine months later, I heard she was in hospital having my kid. She wasn't pleased to see me but at least she let me hold the baby. He was hours old, an ugly little brute, but improved later.

She let me visit from time to time but on Valentine's Day 1964, I turned up and found them gone, no forwarding address.

1 September 2001

My high-watt glow has dimmed but everyone else is buzzing. Sailing's forgotten; all anyone talks about is the match.

We've had the crème brûlée and are into the coffee. Meg's swapping life stories with a woman from Mildura.

I'm wishing that some time during our eighteen years together I'd found the courage to tell Meg about the kid. It suddenly hits me that he's only a year older than she is. The thing is, when you're hitting thirty-six and fall for a girl fourteen years younger who seems stuck on you, you don't want to do anything that might make her realise the sun doesn't shine from your backside. She'll find that out anyway, but if it's gradual she might simply shrug and let you be. Later might have been better. Maybe it would have improved things, if Meg knew.

For years, she said if a baby happened, it happened and she wasn't going to any clinic so the doctors could tell her it never would. She'd say 'What do they know anyway?' but I'd still catch her looking at me as if it was all my fault. How the hell could I tell her it probably wasn't?

And now, I ask myself, what's the point of raking over barren ground?

7 January 1967

'What nil was it?' undermines everything else and at chucking-out time I decide to go back. My son shouldn't be calling me mister.

'You again? Piss off, for Christ's sake.' She keeps looking behind her, head darting like a nervous blackbird's. 'Go,' she hisses and, like a repeat recording, 'Count yourself lucky.'

But I'm not lucky. The door's almost wrenched from its hinges and the local psychopath appears in its place. I stare at him. He stares at me. We've met before.

'What are you doin' here?'

I don't need to answer. Her face says it all.

He pokes me in the back all the way along the street. 'You bastard,' he keeps saying. 'That's my bird you knocked up.'

I want to say she wasn't his bird at the time but he suddenly drops his soliloquy, yanks me round, lands one on me. Then he lands a few more. In fact he kicks my lights out, dumps me against a parked Cortina.

Someone offers to take me to hospital but I spit out teeth, say I'm fine, crawl to my car, somehow reach home.

I resign from my job. 'Ill health,' I tell them. A few months later, I become a ten-pound Pom. In my head, I call it strategic withdrawal.

1 September 2001

Was not telling Meg strategic withdrawal too?

She's looking at me. 'Penny for them, Charlie,' she says.

'Wondering if you fancy an early night.'

Meg gives me her sunshine smile, eyes vibrant, clear blue, lips parted just so over beautifully white, even teeth. 'You're drunk,' she says. 'But yes please.'

And I know coming to Australia was the best thing I ever did because though it took a while to find my feet and longer to find her, it brought me my golden girl.

I give the waitress an outrageous tip, say goodnight to our fellow sailors. 'Beat you round the cans tomorrow,' I say.

A few laugh and respond with 'You'll need a bloody engine, mate', stuff like that.

It's a longish walk to our mooring. We stumble occasionally, and Meg laughs when we do. It's high-pitched, slightly hysterical but sounds good.

People sit on cabin tops, drinking tinnies. They're talking about footy.

'Great result,' we say as we make our way past and someone says, 'The Magpies really stuffed them tonight.'

As I'm reminded that footy here does not refer to soccer, I'm nearly pitched headlong by a mooring line some idiot's stretched over the path. I wish I'd thought to bring a torch.

However, we reach our boat without mishap. I give in to an urge to take Meg in my arms and kiss her the way I used to do when she was twenty-two and fresh in my heart.

'Wow, Charlie, what's got into you?' she says and I know that if I could see them in all this darkness, her eyes would have that old sparkle.

In the dim glow from a bedside lamp, we make love like we did in the old days, thrashing about the tiny cabin, banging against the fibreglass hull. Afterwards, I'm gasping far more than Meg and for a moment she looks concerned. I grin and she relaxes.

'Well, if that won't do it, nothing will,' she says.

It takes me a moment to realise that Meg still carries the dream in her head and I know I have to tell her, finally tell her, because it's never going to go away.

I take two deep breaths.

But it could still be me, I'm thinking. Without tests, no one can say for sure.

Then the voice of my erstwhile child steals into my head: 'What nil was it, mister?'

'Five, son,' I tell him. 'Five.'

He grins, satisfied, and I finally understand it's not the knowing that's important. England won in spite of the odds because, like little George all those years ago, they believed.

Forty's not too old, not these days.

Meg snuggles against me, eyes closed, lips curled into a childlike smile. Moments later, her shoulders jerk and her eyes open. There's a hint of fear in them, as if she feels she's stepped over a forbidden boundary. Then she says, 'Let's keep everything crossed, Charlie.'

'Everything crossed,' I say.

She nods, closes her eyes again. Her hand seeks mine, our fingers entwine, squeeze against each other. In my head, my heart, in the core of me, the possibility of the impossible takes hold.

While the Sand Shifts

My grandmother believed in magic. Not the hocus-pocus wizardy stuff; hers was a more homespun variety in that she claimed to be able to see things that weren't there. She was the only grandparent I had left and Dad always called her an old witch, even though she was his own mother. Mom said he was just biased. I didn't know what biased meant then but that didn't really matter because soon afterwards Dad went to live with somebody else. I was a few weeks short of eleven years old.

A lot of things changed for Mom and me then. First, we moved to a smaller house in a neighbouring community. Second, she got a job so I could attend a private school. It was close to where my grandmother lived and I'd go to her house after school and wait for Mom to pick me up when her shift finished.

There'd been an argument about the school a few days before Dad left but I don't think that's the reason he went. They must have been discussing what was to happen to me because Mom suddenly yelled that she'd rather die than send me to any public school in Boston. Dad bawled back, 'Then you can pay the goddamn fees yourself.'

Dad didn't look anything like his mother. She was tall and gaunt, wore her hair in a bun and had half-frame, schoolmarm spectacles. Her face looked so serious I didn't dare call her Gran until it had gotten used to smiling.

The smiling began to happen when she caught me with my fingers crossed. 'That's to make your dad call here, isn't it?' she said and I nodded, my cheeks feeling like they'd been torched. Maybe she is a witch after all, I thought. Then she said my dad hadn't shown his face at her door since his father died and she reckoned he wasn't about to start now. She hugged me a lot after that and we became friends.

Months became years and I travelled from fifth to eighth grades fatherless and almost without tears. Shortly before I was fifteen, Mom transferred me to a Catholic high school, private of course. It was boys only and I didn't really like that but Mom said, 'It will concentrate that mind of yours on what matters.'

She started working extra shifts.

One December afternoon, during my first term at the new school, I was standing at my grandmother's living room window, gazing outside. It was a half-holiday, for something like the founder's birthday. I was daydreaming as usual and jumped through my skin a little when I heard Gran speaking about an inch behind my ears.

'If you could look through this window into the sands of time,' she said in a dreamy, faraway sort of voice, 'back to the days when my own father was young, you'd see a fine sailing ship. Four high masts packed with white sails crisping with the wind.'

She took an old hourglass from a dresser behind her then rummaged through a drawer and drew out a silver dollar, blackened with age. She pressed the dollar into my palm then set the hourglass on the windowsill so the sand began to trickle from the upper to the lower glass.

'Hold the dollar tightly,' she said, 'and while the sand shifts, feel the silver's power. Watch for those sails and maybe you will see.'

When I was very young, Mom told me to take these stories with a pinch of salt. She didn't explain what I should do with the salt but eventually I realized she meant I shouldn't believe everything my grandmother told me. Well, I didn't believe everything – for instance, like when Gran said my dad wouldn't come back – but mostly I wanted to believe her. And often when I didn't, I'd pretend that I did.

So I let my eyes grow heavy and allowed her words to swim around in my head. I imagined the window changing from its two big sheets of glass into many panes. I counted them: sixteen in all. And beyond the house, my mind removed the intervening streets, and in the harbour I now overlooked, a harbour bare of the mark of today, I saw a tall ship riding low in the water, and a small boat, a pinnace, carrying men ashore.

The pinnace tied up to a quay and the men disembarked. One, taller than the rest, with a great mat of tawny beard, walked up a long cobbled roadway towards the house. On his shoulder he carried a canvas bag, and as he got closer I heard him singing a song I knew: 'Farewell Spanish Ladies'.

My grandmother's face became radiant as footsteps clicked outside her door and her mouth opened in anticipation as the great round handle began to turn, its latch groaning against its catch until it was free.

But when the door was finally open, there was no sea captain waiting outside, no cobblestones to be seen, only the block-paved driveway that had been there when I arrived. And on it stood my mother's silver Beetle.

'Hi, you two,' she said as she sailed into the room with a flurry of coat and skirts. 'I swapped my shift and left early. It's threatening snow.'

As she hugged goodbyes, Gran whispered into my ear. 'You saw. Didn't you?'

As I nodded, her smile reached inside me, warming me against the chill that was sweeping in from outside.

The sky was yellow as we drove off and long before we reached home, the snowfall had begun, a few flakes at first then a thickening into large, regular ones that made it difficult to see our way.

On the journey, I thought about the bearded sailor. When my own father was young, Gran had said, and this man wasn't young. I figured she must have meant when he was my age, for she knew I could only see with a boy's eyes and mind. If that was so, then the man I saw must have been her grandfather. That would make the ship right too, for I knew from school that the sailing clippers would have been gone by the time her father became a man.

It was far more likely, though, I decided, that I'd simply dreamed up images from books I'd grown up with; tales of tall ships and the sea, like *Masterman Ready*.

In our community, ten miles or so west of Boston, neighbours were busy shovelling snow from their drives. One, Eddy Mulcahan, was halfway through clearing ours. His face shone as he saw Mom get out of her VW and he waved a hand near his ear in a casual salute.

'That's most considerate of you, Eddy,' Mom said, putting on a voice that sounded like she was licking cream.

Eddy was almost as bad. He wouldn't look up at Mom but stared at her feet, at the light suede shoes that were showing dark patches where the snow had seeped inside. I imagined him wishing he could suck them dry. His face was turning ruddier by the second. Perhaps it was because of the cold or maybe he knew what I was thinking.

'Why, Mrs Barr,' he said, 'it's nothing.'

Mom switched on a smile I hadn't seen in a long while. It was the one she used to have when Dad told her she was the prettiest girl in all the world. She'd worn it for me once, when my old school awarded me a prize for something, I've forgotten what for. I forget a lot of things.

'Oh, it's something, Eddy,' Mom said.

She still had the smile when we went in the house and it seemed to increase in the warmth there. That evening she baked my favourite choc-chip cookies.

When I went outside next morning, the night's snowfall had already been cleared from our drive. On either side, it was piled as high as my shoulders. It was Saturday and, although the snowplough crews had been out, I was glad Mom didn't have to drive to work today.

'Hey, Jimmy.' It was Eddy Mulcahan, grinning from the cab of his pickup, parked in the road outside his house, two away from ours.

'Hey, Eddy.'

Eddy got out of his pickup and, kicking snow aside in a way I guessed was meant to look casual, walked over to me.

'Some fall, huh?' he said, nodding at the walls of snow.

'I guess so.'

Eddy's grin widened and he clapped me on the shoulder. It wasn't a hard blow but I recoiled as if it was. My feet slipped and nearly tipped me onto the concrete. Eddy seemed not to notice.

'Your mom in?'

I'd intended to shrug but she was already at the door, gazing with a syrupy smile at the swept driveway.

'Why, Eddy, you've been so busy. You didn't have to…'

I felt sick as I watched her, wanted to wipe that look right off her face.

Eddy sidestepped past me and posted himself in front of her. 'I was just wondering, Mrs Barr, if you and Jimmy might like to come sledding.' He cocked a thumb and gestured towards somewhere roughly behind my right ear. 'There's a bunch of people having fun out on Mousehold.'

I glared at the back of his neck then gritted teeth and glared at my mother.

'That's a lovely gesture, Eddy,' she said.

In summer, Mousehold Hill is a slope of flowering meadow. From the little river that creeps through the valley below, there's a gentle grade for fifty yards then it's about one-in-five to the broad plateau on the top, where girls like to sit and make daisy chains. That day, everything was endless white, reflecting the thin winter sun so effectively that the glare almost burned my eyes.

About forty people were there when we arrived. Most had home-made sleds. Eddy had brought a plastic one. He kept giving it a shove then landing on it full length and laughing as he scrabbled it along, using his hands and feet for snow paddles.

'Hey, Jimmy, this is something else,' he said as my mother looked on with an idiot grin.

After about a half dozen runs broadside along the hill, Eddy offered me a go.

'I don't know,' I said.

'Go on, Jimmy,' Mom said. She was looking at Eddy as she spoke, her eyes passing him signals that wished me out of the way for a while.

I jumped on Eddy's sled and aimed it downhill. Three or four other boys were level with me as I started, but I was losing them within thirty feet. I tucked my head down, kept one eye on the open stretch of riverbank and my feet ready to brake if I looked like hitting the trees. The runners whistled through the snow and I felt a surge of what I suppose was adrenalin but I told myself it was my grandmother's magic.

There were skaters on the frozen river, tracing circles as I hurtled towards them. They took no notice of me until it looked as if I was about to join them.

As I dragged both feet in the snow, there were shouts of 'Hey, kid, watch it' and I saw the skaters move aside in a hurry.

The sled might have stopped in time but I got this crazy idea I could shoot right across the river and land on the far bank. So I lifted my feet and gave wild banshee whoops as I hurtled towards my take-off point. I guess I must have had a huge grin too. Then suddenly a runner hit something hard, a root or maybe a stone, and the sled rose in the air at one side and tipped me into virgin snow.

Back on top of the slope again, I watched Eddy rub his hands together and wink at my mother before he launched himself downhill.

'I'll show you how it's done, Jimmy,' he said. 'Wish me luck, Mrs Barr.'

'Oh, Caroline, please, Eddy,' Mom said.

With his legs pumping like crazy pistons, Eddy gave himself a tremendous flying start and the sled careered away. His head was bobbing. He never tried to brake at all but carried on over the river bank.

He didn't make it to the other side and the sound of breaking ice echoed like a firecracker around the little valley.

Mom's hand flew to her mouth. 'Oh dear, oh no,' she said. She started to laugh.

Eddy's arms were spinning like a pair of windmills. The rest of him was in the water. The skaters were on the bank, removing their skates and giving Eddy the occasional finger. The man himself was scrabbling across the remaining ice as if he didn't trust it to stay intact for one second longer. The tail end of his sled was up in the air, its nose anchored into the riverbed. I'd had my feet sucked into that glutinous sludge more than a few times over the summers. It stank like anything.

Instead of letting Eddy take his river stench home, my mother insisted he brought it into our house. 'No, Eddy,' she said. 'I feel responsible for what happened.'

Why? I thought. If he wants to put on a damn fool show, that's his problem, not yours. Then I realised she meant there was something about her that made Eddy act like that. It was her way of telling him that was okay.

She borrowed his house keys and went to fetch him dry clothes while he used our shower. All I could think of was her running her fingers through Eddy's drawers, picking out stuff she had no business to have her hands on.

She came back with navy-blue chinos, a blue shirt, boots and the other stuff Eddy needed. He half opened the bathroom door and she handed the clothes to him. When Eddy was dressed, she sat him by our fireside with a mug of coffee and got our washing machine busy on his dirty clothes. Then she poured herself coffee and sat beside him.

'Eddy,' she said, 'you should wear blue more often.'

Eddy preened himself like some prize peacock and Mom stretched back and stuck her chest out. Eddy's eyes nearly left their sockets. I went to my room and stared out the window. Even the snow looked dirty now.

Eddy stayed around all day and he and my mother were drinking whiskey together when I went to bed.

Something woke me. I'd been dreaming about rats scratching in the attic the way they used to in our old house in Wellesley. Two-thirty-three, said my bedside clock in bright green LED. Then I heard my mother groaning.

I got up and opened my door. Along the corridor a thin shaft of light fanned out from the living room. Mom's groans came from that direction too. I ghosted towards them.

The living room door was a fraction ajar and somewhere behind it Mom was going, 'Oh, oh, oh.'

I thought of calling out 'Is everything okay?' but decided it might be wiser to look first.

Mom was on the floor, skirt up over her waist, and Eddy Mulcahan had his face buried between her thighs. Mom's groans stopped like they'd been sliced through with a razor. She was staring straight at me. Her eyes looked like they wanted to scream.

I retreated to my room, fast. Nobody, nothing, followed me, not even whispers. I sank my face in my pillows, tried to revive my dream about the rats.

When I woke, a hard rain was pelting my windows. Outside, the snow was turning to slush. I washed and dressed, got myself some cereal. While I was in the kitchen, my mother came in. Her face was flushed but there was a hard edge to her lips. She looked as if she'd been up a long time.

'I'd rather you hadn't seen what you did, Jimmy,' she said, 'but I'm not going to apologise, no way. Anyway, you shouldn't have been sneaking around in the middle of the night.'

'I thought you were being murdered.' I pulled a face. 'It was disgusting.'

'It might not be what your biology books teach but it's what men and women do together. It's time you learnt that, Jimmy.'

'But you did it with him.'

'Your father's been gone a long time, Jimmy.'

I could see she wasn't going to see things my way so I left her and went to check if Eddy was still in the house.

I'd no sooner decided the house was Mulcahan-free when somebody rang the front doorbell then hammered on the door itself.

My mother rushed from the kitchen. 'Oh, God,' she said when she opened the door.

My grandmother's prediction was wrong. My dad had come back. He looked as if he'd been crying.

'How did you…?' Mom said.

'Find your address? Better to ask how the hell my mother knew mine. Can I come in, Carrie?' Dad didn't wait for an answer but stepped right into the house.

Outside, a scared-looking face with dark eyes and pale hair was staring out from the windows of a Lexus parked at the bottom of our drive.

It seemed Gran had collapsed about the time I was falling off Eddy's sled. A neighbour had been with her and called 911.

Dad said Gran had regained consciousness that night and told the hospital where to find him. It was a long drive, he said, but he didn't mention where from. Gran talked to him for a good hour then smiled, lay back and died. I was expecting him to tell me it happened at precisely two-thirty-three in the morning but he said it was a few strokes after midnight.

The day after Gran's funeral, I was in her living room again. Dad was there too. And Alice. She was the girl I'd seen in his car. She wasn't the one he'd left us for.

Dad and I had done the awkward stuff – the hugging and him saying I mustn't think he didn't love me – this from the man who never remembered any of my birthdays after my tenth and obviously thought Christmas was just a word. When Mom dropped me off, there'd been a brief closeness between her and him, a huddled conversation.

I heard Mom saying, 'No, really?' a dozen times then she'd left for work. 'Because I need to earn the money,' she'd snapped when Dad asked her why she couldn't stay too.

Dad had scarcely spoken since then, just slumped in Gran's armchair, chewed idly at his fingers. Alice had her back towards us; she was scanning the shelves on Gran's dresser.

I slid the upper sash of Gran's window down and filled my lungs with cold Atlantic air. Below, motor cruisers strutted towards their berths by the waterfront condos.

My eyes were stinging but the tears were locked in. With all that shitty magic of Gran's, she must have known what was to happen, so why didn't she warn me, teach me how to cope without her?

I felt my lips shaking and I wanted to yell out at her but, without warning me, my tear ducts freed themselves and I started blubbing like a kid. I mopped my eyes with my knuckles then leaned out over the open sash, watched the gulls sweeping the bay, guarding the skies.

I reckoned those birds didn't miss much of what was going on. I pictured my tears forming an invisible mist that shimmied past them and spiralled upwards in search of the cloud Gran was floating on. That way she'd know I was sorry.

Dad's voice broke in. 'You okay, son?' He was rubbing his chin, watching me.

'Why did you call Gran an old witch?' I said.

He put on a crumpled face, as if I'd accused him of murder or worse. 'It was a joke, Jimmy. She was my mother. I loved her just as much as you love your mom.'

'Do you love my mom?'

Dad looked away, towards Alice, and at the same moment she turned from examining the dresser. His eyes met hers.

She appeared no older than a high school senior. Eighteen, nineteen at most, Mum had reckoned, twisting her mouth as if there was a nasty taste inside. So Alice had four years on me at the most. I fantasised about such girls sometimes – a lot actually – but I'd never been as close to one as this. I wished we had girls at my school.

Alice had found the hourglass and was running her fingers over it, making the glass squeal. She wore a thin cardigan thing and her nipples were standing out. I couldn't stop myself from staring at them. I wondered if Dad sank his face between her thighs. Alice was looking at me all the while and I guessed she saw right through me.

Dad suddenly turned back to me and I shook my eyes from Alice's breasts. Dad's eyebrows rose. 'Well, well, my boy's growing up,' he said as I burned. 'And the answer to your question, Jimmy, is yes. But not in the way you want. I'm with Alice now.'

Alice was smiling at me as if she wanted my approval.

A hard knot of anger twisted in my gut and I walked over to her and snatched the hourglass from her hands. 'That's mine,' I said. 'Gran gave it to me.'

I reached out to replace it on its shelf, expecting Alice to move aside. She stayed exactly where she was, so I couldn't fail to touch her breasts.

And if it wasn't true I wouldn't have believed it, but she squeezed my dick on the way.

'Excuse me,' I said but Alice stayed where she was. I was still holding the hourglass and I stood there for a moment, insides fluttering, looking down at it. Then something made me open the one dresser drawer which was not fronted by Alice. It contained the silver dollar and I took that out and returned to the window, placed the hourglass on the sill.

'That's not all she gave you, Jimmy.' Dad was standing at my shoulder the way Gran used to and I hadn't heard him coming either.

I slid the dollar into my pocket.

'This house,' Dad said. 'She left it to you and me. Jointly. Now what are we going to do about that?'

I forgot what he'd said about him and Alice. I had a wild, surging hope that he, Mom and I could all live together here and Mom could be free for ever from Eddy Mulcahan and six-dollars-an-hour slavery at the diner.

'You see,' Dad said, 'Alice is expecting my baby. We need to realise the money from my share of this house.'

I turned back to my window, clasped the silver dollar and relaxed but Gran's spell wouldn't work. I squeezed my eyes shut and silently begged her to help.

When I opened them again, I saw the desired sixteen panes of glass before me and, outside, a tall ship coming into the old harbour. It was festooned with gaily-coloured flags, as if there was something to celebrate.

'He'll play fair with you, Jimmy,' I heard Gran's voice saying. 'He knows I'm a witch. He knows what I can do.'

The ship was alongside the wharf now; men scurried about, securing lines to quayside bollards. The tall man with the thicket of beard stepped ashore. He was carrying something that looked like the bellows we used at home.

The man stopped below Gran's window then strapped the bellows beneath an arm and began to pump them. Then I realised they were part of a musical instrument, something like the uilleann pipes I'd heard at school concerts, except this had just a single pipe instead of half a dozen or so. As his fingers danced, the sweetest, most enchanting music I had ever heard began to fill the air. It sounded Irish yet not Irish. And he was gazing up at me.

I felt as if I was suddenly twice my weight. He kept weaving that melody, drawing me into it. I thought of the Pied Piper of Hamelin town.

Then I saw that he was looking past, not at, me and I realised the heaviness was only Gran leaning into me in the way she used to, her arm encircling my shoulder. I recalled a tale she used to tell me about the Isles of the Blest, a land where no one ages and no one dies. That's where the ship was bound, I reckoned, and the piper had come to call her away, to sail with him there aboard that fine vessel.

The pressure on my back was transformed into an unbearable lightness and somewhere in the breeze gusting across the bay I fancied I heard Gran breathe a fading 'Goodbye'.

'Were you listening to me, Jimmy?'

The music had stopped and through the window I could see only present-day things. I turned and saw Dad's face. It seemed to be pleading with me.

'Does Mom know about this?'

'She said it was your decision.'

Something unsettling shivered through me. I'd never had a real decision to make.

'I won't cheat you, Jimmy.'

'I know. Gran just said.'

Dad smiled at that but his eyes looked more than a little scared. 'See, Jimmy, I told you she was an old witch.'

'A good one, though.'

'Yeah, a good old witch.'

The front door rattled and Dad started. Then Mom walked in and he released a long sigh. Mom seemed breathless. She raised an eyebrow at Dad. He nodded back.

'So what do you think, Jimmy?' Mom said.

I looked at Dad, saw him, really saw him, for the first time. Memories

I'd long suppressed blew into my thoughts like the ocean wind: Dad smacking me when I was a baby just because I cried in the night; him locking five-year-old me in the cellar for wetting the bed; him hitting Mom in the hall and me jumping onto his back from halfway up the stairs, missing and knocking myself out. That had saved Mom from the beating. Me too, I suppose. It wasn't long before he left us.

It was hard to equate that man with this but it came to me that playing the bully and chasing girls half your age were part of the same thing. Eddy Mulcahan might act like a kid but Dad was a serial one. There'd be another girl after Alice, and always another, until the day he found himself with nobody, with nothing at all. But I knew even that would not change him and that I didn't want him back.

If Eddy Mulcahan was what Mom wanted, then why shouldn't she have him? At least he was kind, and besotted with her. Maybe he'd grow on me. I wondered how many six-dollars-an-hour my half of Gran's house would cover. Enough, I reckoned, especially if I could persuade Mom to let me enrol at our neighbourhood high.

'Well, Jimmy?' Mom said.

'I think it's okay,' I said.

Dad was all smiles. 'Let's shake on it,' he said and we did: he, Mom, and I.

Alice hadn't moved from her place at the dresser. I took the hourglass back and stood it in its spot among the dust.

'Thank you,' Alice whispered.

I managed to avoid bodily contact this time and I persuaded myself that I'd imagined her touching me before, that it was only my wishful thinking. After all, I'd inherited Gran's imagination, so I had no way of telling if what I saw, felt or heard was ever really true.

I wondered if Mom knew about Alice's baby. Either way, I didn't see the kid being a part of my life.

Acknowledgements

'Letting Paddy Fly' was published in *Carve Magazine*.

'I Saw You Dance at Radio City' was broadcast on BBC Radio.

'Who Will Look After the Roses?' and 'How Long Have You Been Sleeping With Freud?' were published in *Southern Ocean Review*.

'Stratherran No More' was published in *Copperfield Review*.

'For a Yellow Jersey' was published in *World Wide Writers Magazine*, UK, and won their £3,000 Award and Gold Medal for Best Short Story of the Year.

'Dead Chrysanthemums' was published in *Eclectica* and shortlisted for the *Best of Eclectica* anthology.

'Watching the Faces' was published in *Amarillo Bay*.

'Priest in Kilvarnet' and 'Finding Indigo' were published in the *Chance Encounters* anthology (Deakin University Press).

'Is Summer Coming Early?' was published in *Cadenza*.

'Then There Was the Music' was published in the *Border Land* anthology (Deakin University Press).

'Eamon Bunion's Christmas Cracker' and 'While the Sand Shifts' were published in *Buzz Words Magazine*.

'Scorpio Scorpio' was published in *Peninsular Magazine*.

'Power To the Lonely', 'White Bikini Bottoms' and 'What Nil Was It, Mister?' are all new, unpublished stories.